"Uh, I Don't Mean to Disturb You, Lady,"

the cab driver said apologetically, "but do you know anybody that drives a fancy little sports car, maybe something like a Ferrari? Whoever it is has been on our tail ever since we hit the expressway."

"Why, no," Jordan answered, turning in her seat to peer out the grimy back glass. "I don't even know anyone in Los Angeles. . . ."

A feeling very close to jubilation rushed through her even before she spotted the cream-colored sports car.

Her smile widened as she met the driver's puzzled gaze in the rearview mirror. "It's okay," she told him. "It's just a friend of mine. I was expecting him."

DONNA McDOWELL

is an avid reader of mysteries, spy thrillers, cookbooks, historicals, and most of all . . . romances. She reports that "Reading hundreds of well-written, beautifully drawn love stories inspired me to try to write one of my own. I can only hope my attempt is a credit to those inspirations."

Dear Reader:

SILHOUETTE DESIRE is an exciting new line of contemporary romances from Silhouette Books. During the past year, many Silhouette readers have written in telling us what other types of stories they'd like to read from Silhouette, and we've kept these comments and suggestions in mind in developing SILHOUETTE DESIRE.

DESIREs feature all of the elements you like to see in a romance, plus a more sensual, provocative story. So if you want to experience all the excitement, passion and joy of falling in love, then SILHOUETTE DESIRE is for you.

Karen Solem
Editor-in-Chief
Silhouette Books

DONNA McDOWELL
September Winds

Silhouette Desire
Published by Silhouette Books New York
America's Publisher of Contemporary Romance

SILHOUETTE BOOKS
300 E. 42nd St., New York, N.Y. 10017

Copyright © 1985 by Donna McDowell
Cover artwork copyright © 1985 by Scott Gladden

Distributed by Pocket Books

ISBN: 0-373-05204-9

First Silhouette Books printing April, 1985

10 9 8 7 6 5 4 3 2 1

All of the characters in this book are fictitious. Any resemblance to actual persons, living or dead, is purely coincidental.

Silhouette, Silhouette Desire and
colophon are registered trademarks of the publisher.

America's Publisher of Contemporary Romance

Printed in the U.S.A.

BC91

To my husband, Raymond Louis,
for the belief that I could,
and the support to let me try.
To my daughter, Shannon, "Mom's little helper."
To Mother, LaVell, and Carol for always being there.

1

If I were a woman of impulse, Jordan Sinclair thought, I would tell Steven Durrell what he could do with his movie deal and his foul-smelling cigar and be on my way back to New Mexico.

But Jordan had not gotten where she was by giving in to foolhardy impulses. That, and the knowledge that her anger was not directed solely toward Durrell kept her seated and silent, her inner turmoil well hidden from all but the most discerning eyes.

"I've always said timing was everything, especially in the movie business. Take my last picture, for example—"

You take it, she thought wrathfully, listening to the producer's drone, I don't want it. In fact, I don't want any part of this. I should be home in front of my typewriter. I don't belong here; I don't want to belong here. I should have known better than to get involved in this deal. This isn't my world. What am I doing here listening to this anyway?

For the past five hours, she had been wined, dined and

shown the sights; she had done everything but what she had come to California to do. Now, finally seated in Durrell's studio office, she did her best to subdue her impatience as his lengthy monologue on the fine art of movie making threatened to stretch even longer.

Of course there was a method to Durrell's madness, she reflected, watching him wave his arm in the air to illustrate another point. He was stalling.

A young man for the position he held, Steven Durrell was this week's fair-haired boy in Hollywood. Every motion picture he'd produced in the previous three years had turned to solid gold at the box office. He was now turning that production genius to a "made for television" movie, and Jordan's book was the vehicle in which he'd chosen to make his television debut.

There was, however, a small hitch in his plans, Jordan thought wryly, studying his thin, expressive face. And she was the hitch.

She shifted her attention to the only other person in the room and met the knowing gaze of her agent, Ryan Collier. Ryan 's lips twitched with suppressed laughter as he correctly read the expression on her face, and Jordan knew that he recognized Durrell's delaying tactics as well.

"And everyone wants more money. If it's not the actors, it's the director, and if it's not the director, it's the writers—"

With great effort she pulled her attention back to the producer's monologue, grimacing inwardly as he enumerated the high costs associated with producing a quality film. Jordan tried to concentrate on his words, but her thoughts kept drifting, straying to a fourth person who should have been there but was noticeably absent.

She had requested this meeting today and had specifically asked that Lance Rutledge also attend. Obviously, he felt he had better things to do with his time. Anger bubbled up in her chest. He had written that God-awful screenplay—

It took a moment or two for Jordan to realize that the room had suddenly gone quiet. Durrell, rummaging through his pockets for a match to relight his cigar, offered a slight pause in his rambling dissertation, and Jordan would have never forgiven herself if she had failed to take advantage of it.

"Mr. Durrell," she said into the sudden silence, allowing him no opportunity to reclaim the floor. "I want to thank you for a very interesting day. Ryan and I appreciate the time you have taken from your busy schedule to show us around and acquaint us with the inner workings of a production studio. However, we have both traveled quite a distance today in order to discuss the screenplay you sent me last week and, speaking for myself, I'd like to get this resolved as quickly as possible. I have commitments at home I need to get back to."

Ryan agreed at once. "Yes, I'm due back in New York tomorrow night. I'd like to have the matter settled before I go."

"All right." Durrell's gaze narrowed. "Let's discuss the screenplay." Turning to Jordan, he inquired bluntly, "What did you think of it?"

"I hated it," she stated without hesitation.

"Lance said you would," he returned calmly, leaning back in his chair.

Momentarily stunned, she could do nothing but stare at the man as though he had suddenly sprouted a third eyeball. "Lance . . . Lance Rutledge said I would hate it?"

"Yes. He was quite certain you would." He flicked the ashes of his cigar in a nearby ashtray.

Jordan could feel a pressure building in her chest. "If he knew I would hate it, why did he write it like that?"

"Because I told him to," Durrell answered. "It needed some pizzazz."

"Pizzazz!" She almost choked on the word. "You had Lance Rutledge write that—that piece of junk because my book needed pizzazz?" She stared at him in disbelief.

"Miss Sinclair, try to understand." Durrell's voice was suddenly placating. "Today's television audience is extremely demanding. To be successful, a show the length of a miniseries has to incorporate a combination of all the popular entertainment trends such as humor, drama, romance, mystery, pathos and so on. Four hours of uninterrupted sentimentality would quickly pall."

"I don't buy that," Jordan said, rising from her chair. "In case you've forgotten, *A Private War* stayed on the best-seller charts for twenty-six weeks. I don't believe readers thought of it as 'uninterrupted sentimentality.' "

Durrell also rose to his feet. "Miss Sinclair, surely I don't have to point out the obvious differences between telling a story with the written word and telling a story with celluloid images."

"Maybe there's not as much difference between the two as you think, Mr. Durrell." Her voice mirrored her contempt. "I can't count the number of good books that have been mutilated when reproduced on the 'silver screen.' Why is it the producer and director always think they know more about the story than the writer? Do they never stop to consider that the reading audience that made a book popular will be the same audience to see it as a movie?"

"I'm afraid that's an overly simplistic summation." His tone was frankly patronizing. "The transition from best seller to box office is extremely difficult. There are many things involved in producing a film that a writer never has to worry about. Locations, for example. The writer has complete and free access to any location in the world. It doesn't cost any more to write about a sheik in the middle of the Arabian desert than it does the boy next door."

"I understand the production costs, Mr. Durrell," Jordan said stiffly. "But you had complete scenes of my book obliterated that had nothing to do with production costs. I expected some changes, and I knew there would be some additions and deletions in the scenes to make it adaptable to the screen, but I didn't expect to see my characters suddenly change personalities and the plot switch directions!"

"I think we might get more accomplished here if we all sat down and discussed this reasonably," a quiet voice interjected. "I don't think yelling at each other will accomplish anything."

Both Jordan and Durrell turned to stare at Ryan in surprise. They had been so absorbed in their private tug-of-war that, for a moment, they had forgotten his presence in the room. Now, nimbly uncoiling his long frame from a rather small side chair, he, too, rose to his feet.

He had been a silent observer of their heated exchange, neither interrupting nor contributing, only listening. Now he met Jordan's stormy blue gaze with the calm reassurance of his own, acknowledging and accepting her silent plea for him to intercede. She trusted Ryan totally, and his almost imperceptible nod eased her tension somewhat. She sat back in her chair, watching Durrell warily as he did the same.

Jordan swallowed hard on the anger and frustration churning up in her throat. It was obvious she was too close to the matter, too emotionally involved to be effective in any kind of bargaining situation. It might be better if she kept quiet, she admitted grudgingly.

"All right, Collier, let's discuss it," Durrell said, his tone mocking.

"I believe Miss Sinclair's first and foremost concern is the changes made in the plot line and major characters," Ryan began, choosing to ignore Durrell's sardonic inflection. He was not one of New York's most successful agents by accident. He had dealt with men like Steven Durrell too often to be intimidated now. "These changes, made without Miss Sinclair's consent or prior knowledge, drastically alter the mood and tone of the original story line, which we were promised would remain essentially intact."

"For example?" Steven Durrell prompted.

"For example," Ryan continued, *"A Private War* is the story of Rachel Waterman, the victim of a brutal husband, a heartless family and a status-conscious society. Rachel was a battered wife who had to learn to put her world back together and make a life for herself on her own. But in your adaptation, Rachel has gone from victim to masochist, a playgirl-type personality, with none of the inner strength and beauty of the original character."

"I think that's a rather severe appraisal, Collier," Durrell bristled. "I'll admit I injected a little color into Rachel's character, but certainly not to the extent that she becomes masochistic. Viewers want realism, and you'll have to admit that as she was originally created, Rachel was just a bit too good to be true."

"But it was true," Jordan cried, forgetting her own resolve to remain silent. Feeling both pairs of masculine eyes on her, she hurriedly explained, "I spent months researching that character. I interviewed hundreds of battered wives, studied case histories, talked to dozens of psychologists, counselors, social workers, police investigators and clergymen. I knew that character inside and out before I ever put her on paper."

A stark silence followed her outburst. She glanced from one face to the other, trying to read their expressions. Ryan's reflected sympathy and support, but Durrell's expression was closed and unreadable.

She regretted her momentary loss of control and silently prayed that neither man would inquire too deeply into the cause for it. Things were not going the way she had planned at all. She had intended to come to California and resolve this matter quickly, professionally and unemotionally, but she had not succeeded. It had been more than two years since she had written that book, the intended catharsis of putting it down on paper not bringing the relief she had sought, and she was forced to admit that she was still as emotionally involved with it today as she had been the day she had started writing it. Somehow, some way, she would have to get past that involvement.

Steven Durrell was the first to break the strained silence. "I think the best thing to do at this point would be to set up a meeting with Lance. I'm sure we can work out any details that we're in disagreement over."

"Mr. Durrell." Jordan could not disguise her impatience. "We're talking about more than details here."

Ryan quickly intervened. "I think what Jordan is trying to say is that we feel the series could be just as powerful if it followed the original story line. There are lots of women out there who will identify with Rachel's situ—"

"I don't make documentaries," Durrell interrupted impatiently.

"And I don't put my name on trash!" Jordan exclaimed. "I'm beginning to think the only reason you bought the rights to my book was so that you could play on its current popularity. You just want to pin my title on that . . . that fiasco you call a screenplay. I don't believe you ever had any intentions of keeping the original story line intact." All of her determination to leave the discussion strictly a business matter, devoid of sentimentality and emotionalism, was forgotten in the heat of the moment. Rising to her feet, she heard a betraying tremor in her voice as she continued. "Well, it's no deal. I won't let you do that to my book. You can just forget about making *A Private War* into anything!"

"I'm afraid I can't do that, Miss Sinclair." Durrell's voice was deceptively calm as he rose to face her. "In case you've forgotten, we have a contract."

"I haven't forgotten," she answered icily. "I believe it's the same contract that gives me final approval of the screenplay. Well, you're crazy if you think I'll ever approve that garbage."

"It also gives us the option to rewrite," he reminded her tightly, his thin, almost pointed features appearing even sharper. "I've already sold the deal to the network. You're not backing out on me now."

Jordan's fury was in full swing now. "Just watch me."

Durrell leaned over the desk. "Tradewind Productions has an excellent legal department, Miss Sinclair."

She met his gaze head on. "Then sue me."

"Don't think I won't. If you think I'll let you pull a stunt like this, think again. You'll be in court so fast it'll make your head swim."

"I think we're getting away from the real issue here," Ryan Collier's voice sliced into the tension-filled air, effectively forestalling whatever angry retort Jordan had been intending to make. "I still believe there is a reasonable solution to the problem if we sit down and discuss it sensibly."

"You'd be better off explaining that to your client," Durrell jeered.

Ryan ignored the insult. "It's getting late, and we're all tired. Perhaps we should call it a day. But I do think your suggestion that we meet with Lance Rutledge and discuss our differences on the script is an excellent idea. Do you think you could arrange a meeting for sometime tomorrow?"

"That shouldn't be any problem." Durrell reached for the console sitting on his desk and quickly punched out a number. "I'll give him a call and see what time would be convenient for him."

He returned the receiver to its cradle several moments later. "No answer," he told them. "I'll try again later. His office is out at his house. He's normally easy to reach."

Ryan nodded, then turned to Jordan. "Why don't we go on to the hotel?" he asked. "I'm sure you'd like a chance to rest and freshen up before dinner." His gaze swung back to Durrell. "You can call us there after you've reached Rutledge, can't you?"

"Of course. That's a good idea," Durrell agreed with unconcealed relief. It was obvious that Jordan's presence was no more pleasing to him than his was to her. "I'll have my driver take you."

"That's not necessary," Ryan began immediately, sensing Jordan's disapproval of the idea. "We can easily call a taxi."

Durrell's laugh was derisive. "Sorry, old man, but this is

L.A., not New York. There's not a cab on every corner here. Besides, I won't be using the car for a while anyway."

A few minutes later Jordan found herself seated in the back of Steven Durrell's gleaming black limo, speeding along one of Los Angeles's famous freeways, headed downtown to the hotel where she and Ryan had booked rooms. She glanced about the car, half-amused, half-annoyed. She ran her hand over the dove gray velour upholstery, and let her fingers tinker idly with the control panel beside her armrest.

"I didn't know they still made these things," she whispered to Ryan.

He smiled, lightening his rather somber features. "You don't have to whisper. He can't hear us through the glass partition," he said, nodding toward the driver.

"Good. He probably wouldn't like to hear what I'm about to say about his boss."

Ryan chuckled at her expression, and she felt some of her tension ebbing away. She had known Ryan Collier for almost six years, and in that time, she had never known him to get the least bit rattled, no matter how traumatic or earth-shattering she personally considered the situation to be. He was always cool and confident, with never so much as a hair out of place.

She looked at him now—his long frame conservatively clothed in a suit and vest, his short, sandy blond hair immaculately styled, his shoes shined and his nails manicured—and wondered if he ever relaxed. She tried to picture him in cutoffs and a T-shirt, but could not get past the polished image she was familiar with.

"You know, Ryan, I've known you almost six years now, and I've never known anything to ruffle your feathers. Doesn't anything ever get to you? Don't you ever get mad, I mean really hopping, fighting mad?"

"Sure, everyone does," he answered, slanting her a sidelong glance. "I just don't let it show as much as some people do."

"I know what you're thinking," she admitted ruefully. "I blew it with Durrell by losing my temper." She sighed and watched the city scenery passing by. "I guess I could have handled it better."

"Better still, you could have let me handle it. That's what I'm here for."

She continued to stare out the car window. "I know and I'm sorry. I shouldn't have jumped in like that, but I just couldn't seem to help myself. I promised myself I'd be very cool and professional about this, but he was so smug and . . . patronizing, all my good intentions"—she turned to smile at him—"just seemed to fly out the window."

Ryan reached across the small space that separated them and patted her hands as they lay folded in her lap. "Don't worry about it. Everything's going to work out."

She took a deep breath. "What can we do now?"

"Make them rewrite, of course."

He sounded so confident and unperturbed that she was beginning to wonder if perhaps she wasn't overreacting to the situation. She probably shouldn't have even come to California. Ryan had tried to talk her out of it, assuring her that her presence was not necessary. It was part of his job as her agent, he had pointed out, to handle this type of thing for her. But she had to come. Ryan was a good agent, and she never doubted for one moment that he had her best interests at heart, but he couldn't possibly realize how important this was to her.

"I'm sorry if my being here is a nuisance, Ryan," she told him seriously.

"Nonsense," he answered. "You couldn't be a nuisance if you wanted to. Besides, I'm always glad to see you. I don't know why you don't come to New York more often."

"Because I don't like New York. I've told you that. Why don't you come to Ruidoso more often?"

Ryan's snort was ungentlemanly but explicit, leaving little doubt as to his opinion of the small New Mexico resort community. "Thanks, anyway. But I've grown rather fond of civilization."

She smiled, remembering his one and only visit. He had felt and looked as out of place as she did when she visited New York. "And I suppose you think New York is civilized?"

"At least in New York there's some decent entertainment. The next time you come up, we'll have to do the town up right."

"You keep saying that, but every time I've been there, you've been so busy, I've hardly seen you."

His voice dropped to a husky whisper. "Would you have liked it better if I'd spent more time with you?" he asked, and she recognized the teasing quality of his tone.

Teasing or not, she was uncomfortable with the new direction the conversation had taken and was immensely relieved to see their hotel just ahead. "Behave yourself," she told him, affecting a severe tone. "Otherwise, I'll have my phone taken out and make you come to Ruidoso every time you need to discuss something."

"You wouldn't be so cruel," he answered dramatically, stepping out of the car.

He held out his hand to her and she accepted it, sliding gracefully from the seat to stand beside him. "You wouldn't care to put it to a test, would you?"

She was investigating her room and bath when the phone rang a few minutes later.

It was Ryan. "Durrell just called," he said as soon as she answered. "He wants us to meet him here in the hotel for dinner tonight."

Her refusal died on her lips at his next words. "Lance Rutledge will be there too."

That announcement put a whole new light on the situation, and she suspected that Ryan had known it would. She definitely wanted to meet the well-known screenwriter. She had admired his work for years and had to admit that the only reason she had finally agreed to sell the film rights to *A Private War* was Durrell's promise that Lance Rutledge would write the screenplay. That she had been badly disappointed in that screenplay did not lessen her desire to meet the writer himself.

"What time?" she asked, succumbing.

"Drinks at eight, dinner at nine," Ryan answered. "Why don't I come for you about a quarter to?"

"Fine. I'll be ready." She returned the phone to its cradle and glanced at her watch. Six-fifteen.

Time enough for a relaxing soak, she decided, kicking off her high-heeled sandals and tossing her suit jacket on the bed. And right now, she admitted candidly, she badly needed to relax.

She pulled fresh lingerie from her suitcase, which was open on the bed, and padded quietly to the bathroom, shedding the remainder of her clothes as she went. The hotel had graciously stocked the bath with a small packet of herbal-scented bubble bath, and she poured its contents under the tap and watched the tub fill with delicious-smelling bubbles. She pinned her long, midnight-dark hair on top of her head and stepped gingerly into the water, letting her slender frame sink gratefully into the relaxing depths of the tub. She rested her head against its rim and let the soft, fragrant water wash away the remainder of her tensions.

She shouldn't let the Steven Durrells of this world get to her, she mused, stretching her limbs and wiggling her toes. All that emotional strain and anxiety was hard on the nervous system. She would just have to learn to deal with them with more finesse and less friction. It was much less wearing that way.

Tonight, she resolved, she was going to be charm personi-fied. The producer would never be one of her favorite persons, but arguing with him obviously moved no moun-tains. Perhaps a more subtle form of persuasion was called for. Not that she had a lot of experience in the art of subtle persuasion, her normal method being much more straightforward and direct, but—she smiled as she sank deeper into the bubbles—she supposed one must learn to be adaptable.

By seven-thirty she was ready. She had never been one to fuss and preen in front of a mirror; and although she wanted to look her best, especially tonight, it was not in her nature to spend hours in preparation, reorganizing her features from little jars and bottles. She had decided years ago that one simply did the best with what one had and went on.

She had never been impressed with her looks, having been told since birth that they were nothing to be impressed with. So when she looked at her reflection, she saw nothing particularly exciting about her long, true black hair, often believing its thickness and natural curl were more a liability than an asset. The same was true of her deep, midnight blue eyes. She saw nothing unusual about them, certainly not in their color or shape, or the fact that the lashes surrounding them were as dark and thick as her hair. It never occurred to her that her coloring was striking, and if heads turned when she passed by, she was blissfully unaware.

Ryan arrived right on time and, as Jordan swung the door open, she heard his quick intake of breath and glanced up in time to catch the hunger in his eyes. Laughing, she did a quick pirouette, and her silver blue skirt swished silkily against her ankles.

"You look sensational," he said softly.

Her gaze slid over his dark jacket and crisp white shirt. "You don't look too bad yourself."

"Perhaps I should call Durrell and cancel dinner."

"Oh, no." She smiled, determined to keep the mood light. "I've been looking forward to meeting our famous screenwriter, and I won't let you talk me out of it now."

"All right, but don't say I didn't offer," he returned, stepping aside as she moved to pick up her key from the dressing table and drop it into the velvet interior of her evening bag.

"Shall we go?" she asked, turning back to him.

"Yes, of course." He watched her walk toward him. "Jordan—"

"We'd better hurry, Ryan," she interrupted, sensing what his next words would be. "We don't want to be late."

His expression was one of resignation as he opened the door for her. She had realized several months back that Ryan wanted to deepen their relationship, move it from business to personal, but she had no such desire and hated to see an excellent working relationship ruined.

They were both silent during the elevator ride to the rooftop club and restaurant, and Jordan exhaled a soft sigh of relief as the elevator finally slid to a stop at the top floor. She stepped into the large foyer, catching her breath at the tropical beauty of the decor.

They skirted a tall palm tree growing in the middle of the entrance to the lounge and were immediately met by a seating hostess. Ryan gave her the name of their party.

"Of course. If you'll follow me," she said, leading the way to a table next to the windows.

Now that the meeting was at hand, Jordan felt an odd sensation crawl along the back of her neck and down her spine. She had to admit that she was less wary of Durrell than she had been now that she had met him and recognized his methods, but Lance Rutledge was still an unknown quantity and a famous one at that. After all, what did you say to a person who only four months earlier had won an Oscar for an amazing screen adaptation but had made hash out of yours?

Durrell, on the other hand, must have reached the same conclusion as Jordan, for when he spotted them making their way to the table he immediately rose and came forward to meet them, a smile on his face—the first Jordan had witnessed—and his hand extended. Pleasantries were exchanged before he led them back to the table where a man and a woman were seated, facing the window, their backs to the room. At the sound of their approach, the man pushed back his chair, bent low to whisper something in the woman's ear, then straightened and turned, a smile of greeting on his lips.

His expression altered slightly as his gaze met Jordan's. A flicker of surprise chased briefly across his lean features, and Jordan realized that the same expression must be on her face.

"Jordan Sinclair?" He sounded as shocked as she felt.

"Lance Rutledge?" Was that her voice? Funny, she'd never noticed that squeak before. "You're Lance Rutledge?"

"The same," he answered, watching with interest her prolonged inspection of him. "Oh, oh. Have I had bad press?" A smile lifted one corner of his mouth. "It's lies, all lies. Don't believe a word you've heard or read. I'm really a nice guy."

Her smile came naturally. "I'll try to keep that in mind."

While her mind registered the soft drawl of his words, she was observing his lean, attractive features, his sun-streaked brown hair, his dark eyes and the seductive curve of his generous mouth. Not at all what she'd expected, she mused. Not at all.

Ryan's hand at the small of her back reminded her of his presence. Glancing over her shoulder at him, she smiled apologetically and drew him forward. "Mr. Rutledge, I'd like you to meet my agent, Ryan Collier."

"We've been looking forward to meeting you, Mr. Rutledge," Ryan said, extending his hand. "We've heard a lot about you, of course. Congratulations on the Oscar."

"It's just Lance, and thank you. It was quite an honor. And speaking of honor"—his gaze returned to Jordan— "I've waited a long time to meet *the* Jordan Tyler Sinclair."

"Miss Sinclair, Collier," Durrell suddenly spoke beside them, pulling their attention back to himself and the woman who was still seated at the table. "May I also introduce my wife, Audra."

Jordan and Ryan both acknowledged the introduction to the tiny blonde, who surprised Jordan by shyly admitting that the only reason she had joined them was to meet her.

"I've enjoyed all your works," she confided, "but I thought *A Private War* was the best book I'd ever read. I was the one who showed it to Stevie."

Stevie? Jordan smiled at the pet name and thought how differently she would have pictured Durrell's wife.

"Thank you, Mrs. Durrell. It's always a pleasure to meet a fan."

"Why don't we all have a seat and order a drink?" Durrell suggested, again the gracious host. "I, for one, am really dry."

Lance hastily pulled out the chair he had just vacated. "Here, Collier, take my seat. Jordan and I will sit here by the windows." His hand cupped her elbow as he guided her around the table. "You don't mind if I call you Jordan, do you?"

His warm breath stirred her hair, and she glanced up, surprised to find his face so close to hers. "No, of course not," she told him, but could not silence the small warning bell going off in the back of her head.

They were hardly settled in their seats before the waiter came to take their order, and Jordan debated about whether to order anything alcoholic or not. She wasn't used to drinking and wanted a clear head to deal with the business of this evening. She finally settled on a daiquiri, knowing she would probably never finish it.

"You looked a bit surprised when you first came in this evening," Lance said quietly, near her ear. "Don't I live up to my public image?"

A quick glance across the table confirmed that Ryan was engaged in conversation with Durrell and his wife. She had little alternative but to answer Lance Rutledge's rather leading question.

"Since I don't know what your public image is, I can't say whether you do or not," she answered, matching her tone to his. "But speaking of surprised, you looked a bit startled yourself."

"That just goes to show you what a great actor I am," he replied. "I was really shocked."

"Why in the world would you be shocked at meeting me?" she asked, too self-conscious to admit to the same reaction.

"Let's just say you weren't what I was expecting."

"I'll probably regret asking, but what were you expecting?"

His expression turned reflective for a moment. "I'm not sure," he answered, studying her features thoughtfully. "After I'd read your book, I tried to picture what you'd look like. I agree with Audra. I thought it was one of the best books I'd ever read. But I pictured the author to be someone older, I guess. Tougher, maybe."

"I'm sorry to disappoint you, then."

His dark eyes gleamed as he smiled at her. "Oh, I'm not disappointed," he assured her. "I just wish I'd been better prepared." He shot an accusing glance in Durrell's direction, but the producer was still deep in conversation with Ryan and did not notice the arrows being fired at him. "He could have warned me to expect a tiny"—he paused significantly, letting his eyes travel appraisingly down the length of her petite frame—"raven-haired beauty with the deepest blue eyes"—he paused again, this time to stare deeply into those eyes—"I've ever seen in my life."

Jordan could not prevent the delicate pink that colored her cheeks and laughed lightly to cover her confusion. She was used to men's appraising glances, but was normally able to ignore them. She knew that Lance Rutledge would be hard to ignore under any circumstances, but especially when he chose to be charming and irresistible. She took another quick sip of her drink and tried to decide rationally how to handle the situation. For years, she had believed herself immune to the opposite sex. It had taken Lance Rutledge ten minutes to prove that she wasn't.

"Mr. Rutledge," she began, only to be interrupted.

"Lance," he commanded softly.

"All right. Lance," she said, trying the name experimentally, liking the feel of it on her tongue. "I was under the impression that this was to be a business dinner."

"And you want to discuss the screenplay, right?"

"Right."

"There's not really a lot to discuss, is there?" he asked, picking up his drink and downing a healthy swallow. His question surprised her, but before she could answer, he continued, "I mean, you hated it, didn't you?" She nodded in answer. "That means it goes back for rewrites. What else is there to discuss?" He cocked a dark brow.

Momentarily unbalanced by the directness of his answer, Jordan quickly regained her equilibrium. "Quite a lot, I would think," she answered curtly. "If you liked the book as much as you said, how could you have written that perfectly awful screenplay?"

"Easy." His tone was relaxed, amused. "I was paid to write it the way Durrell wanted it written. I'll get paid again to write it the way you want it written."

"Is that all it means to you? A paycheck?" Her voice was suddenly husky with emotion. "Didn't it bother you to take a good story and write it into that . . . that trash?"

"Nope," he answered in his same casual tone. Ignoring Jordan's sharp intake of breath, he continued, "There was never a doubt in my mind that you were going to reject it. I knew it would never make it to the screen in that form."

Jordan slowly expelled the breath she had been holding and felt like a deflated balloon. She also felt like a fool, and wouldn't have blamed Lance at all if he had taken offense at her callous remarks. She had warned herself over and over about the danger of being too emotionally involved with that book and had repeatedly tried to maintain a detached attitude. It irritated her to know that this was one area of her life that she couldn't control.

She turned to Lance. "I apologize if I offended you." She kept her voice soft, not wanting the others at the table to hear, but she need not have worried. They were still deep in conversation, discussing Durrell's last movie, an Oscar nominee prosaically named *Star Quest.*

When Lance did not comment, she continued hesitantly, "I'm usually not so sensitive about my books, but this one is . . . well, you might say that it's sort of special to me. I didn't want to sell the movie rights to it. The only reason I finally consented was that Durrell said you'd be doing the screenplay." She glanced at him from under her lashes, but his expression gave nothing away. "I had read *All the Long Days* before I saw the movie and I was very impressed. I thought you wrote a beautiful script." There was still no reaction. "Anyway, when Durrell said you'd be the writer, I thought you would do the same sort of job with *A Private War.* I couldn't believe it when Durrell sent me the script last week. I had expected it to be beautiful."

"It will be beautiful," Lance said gently. "That's why I want you to help me on the rewrite."

Jordan's eyes widened in amazement. "Help you?" she repeated, certain that she must have heard him wrong. "I can't help you. I don't know anything about writing a screenplay."

"Sure you can," he insisted patiently. "We'd make a great team. I can teach you everything you need to know about screenwriting and, in turn, you can give me special insight into the characters and story." His voice suddenly dropped to a husky whisper as his gaze made an intimate inspection of her soft features. "After all," he asked softly, "who could know more about Rachel than Rachel?"

2

Jordan could feel the icy fingers of shock clutching at her, but she forced herself to sit perfectly still, not moving, not flinching, even though it took every ounce of her willpower to do so. She refused to let her pain or fear surface. She held her eyes steady, breathing carefully, willing herself to act naturally and not betray herself.

Her lips felt rubbery when she tried to move them, but the rough laugh that escaped them sounded almost natural. "I hate to disappoint you again, Lance, but Rachel is a totally fictional character."

"Is she?" He didn't try to hide his skepticism.

"Yes, she is," she answered forcefully, then shot a quick glance across the table to see if anyone else could hear their conversation. She lowered her voice. "Yes, she is. A lot of time and research went into that character. I interviewed a hundred women or more, and studied each individual case file before I ever committed Rachel to paper. You might say she is a composite of all those women."

"I'm not doubting the research, Jordan," he said in a

serious undertone, his gaze also on the others at the table.
"It shows in the thoroughness of the character and plot
development. But I realized the first time I read the book that
Jordan Tyler Sinclair had to be Rachel. There was so much
depth to her character and her story was told with such
sincerity. It's hard to fake that. Only someone who had lived
that story could have written it." He turned his gaze to her,
and his eyes were gentle. "I take it no one else knows."

She shook her head. "That's because there's nothing to
know, Mr. Rutledge." She laughed lightly. "I must be getting
to be a better writer than I thought if I can make someone as
experienced as yourself believe it so thoroughly."

"You're an excellent writer, one of the best I've ever read,
but you're not that good." He held up a hand when she
would have interrupted. "I don't know what your reasons
are for denying it, but I do know that the author who created
Rachel had inside knowledge that no interviews and no case
files could have provided. As I said before, some things can't
be faked." His tone suddenly softened. "I assume your
reasons for denying it are personal, and I can respect that. It
goes without saying, of course, that I will make no mention
of this discussion to anyone. I can be very discreet."

"I'm relieved to hear that, Lance." She raised her brows
in an expression of mock concern. "I'd hate for everyone to
think you'd lost your mind."

Before Lance could answer, a black-coated waiter suddenly materialized at Durrell's side, informing them that their
table in the dining room was ready.

"I think we're all ready." Durrell's gaze slid around the
table. "Shall we go in?"

Jordan met Ryan's questioning gaze as she pushed her
chair away from the table. His expression told her that he
had seen her in close conversation with Lance and was now
curious, but she had no intention of satisfying that curiosity.
She stepped quickly away from the table, hurrying to follow
the waiter.

Audra Durrell fell into step beside her. "I'm sorry we

didn't get much chance to visit at the table, but when Steven gets to talking about one of his films, he doesn't know when to shut up." She flashed a quick smile. "I've been looking forward to meeting you ever since Stevie said you were coming to California." Her voice dropped to a low whisper. "I'm afraid I'm very jealous of you."

"Whatever for?" Jordan gasped, a quick picture of Steven Durrell leaping into her head. Surely the woman didn't think she could make a play for her husband, did she?

"Your talent." Audra laughed at Jordan's shocked expression. "I've always wanted to be a writer," the petite blonde confided. "I used to daydream about being a famous mystery writer like Agatha Christie or maybe writing a sweeping historical novel like *Gone with the Wind*."

"Then why don't you?" Jordan asked, following the waiter through a maze of tables and greenery.

"I'm not like you, I'm afraid. I don't have the words," the woman confessed. "I guess I was meant to be a reader, not a writer."

The utter simplicity of her admission left Jordan groping for a response. She was saved by the waiter as he came to a stop beside a secluded corner table.

"Perfect," Steven Durrell declared as he joined them. "Just exactly what I ordered. A quiet table with a great view of my favorite city."

Jordan was more careful about the seating arrangements this time, purposely taking a chair next to Audra Durrell. Ryan chose the seat directly across from her, and Lance and Durrell seated themselves at either end. That Lance had chosen to sit at Jordan's immediate right disturbed her, but at least it did not allow for any further private conversation. She had not considered, however, under-the-table conversation.

The waiter held her chair for her, and as she slid her legs under the table, her knee made contact with the solid flesh of another leg. A quick glance at Lance Rutledge confirmed the owner of the knee, the devilish gleam in his night-dark eyes leaving no doubt. The table was not large, but Jordan moved her leg as far as she could without crowding Audra. Lance's knee followed. She slid her leg an extra inch or so, brushing against the silky material of Audra's skirt. Again, Lance's knee followed.

This is crazy! she told herself. Thirty-year-old women do not play footsie under the table. In exasperation, she sat up straight in her chair and fired Lance a withering glance. He returned her look with an innocent smile, and Jordan snapped open her menu. Perhaps the best way to deal with him, she decided crossly, was to ignore him.

But she found that to be a difficult task. By tacit agreement, neither Jordan's book nor the screenplay was discussed over dinner. The topics ranged, instead, from food choices to current politics to the latest Hollywood scandal. And throughout it all, there was the tingling awareness of Lance's knee pressed against hers under the table.

The meal progressed smoothly, and although Jordan was not able to relax completely, she had to admit that the meal was not unenjoyable. The food was excellent and the company stimulating.

When drawn from her shell, Audra Durrell was a warm, friendly person with a sharp mind and a quick wit. Even her husband wasn't so bad when he set out to be agreeable, as he obviously had tonight, and Ryan could always be counted on to be knowledgeable and entertaining. If there was a surprise in the evening, it was Lance Rutledge.

She had already experienced his playboy charm and easy, outrageous humor, but during the course of the evening she was witness to other facets of his personality. She had expected skill and intelligence; they were both evident in his writing. But there was also a gentle side, a compassionate side, that surfaced when Audra mentioned her volunteer work as cochairman of a children's home. Lance's interest was immediate and sincere, and Jordan could almost see the pain in his face as Audra described the condition of some of the children when they arrived at the home. For the first time since dinner had begun, the knee was absent.

Lance kept up a steady barrage of questions that Audra eagerly answered until Steven Durrell laid his hand on her arm just as she was about to launch into another detailed description of one of the center's new projects.

"Darling, I realize how much you enjoy your work at the center," Durrell said quietly, "but our guests may not share your enthusiasm. A children's home is not exactly the most stimulating dinner topic."

"I'm sorry." Audra was instantly contrite. "I didn't realize . . . I mean, I guess I just got carried away."

"My fault, Steve," Lance inserted. "Children are one of my favorite subjects. Did I tell you I'm working with Dina Lambert on the script for a new children's movie?" The knee came back in place.

"No, I hadn't heard," Durrell answered. "She's been out of circulation for a while, hasn't she? Is she still as good at the typewriter as she used to be?"

"Probably better. She's mellowed a lot since the old days." The knee pressed more firmly, and Lance's brown eyes were soft, gentle, as he turned his gaze to Jordan. "Of course, she's nothing to compare with our present company."

Ryan, who had sat quietly through this latest exchange, now leaned forward, his attention directed to Lance. "Speaking of which, Jordan and I were wondering, Lance, if you would be available tomorrow to discuss your screenplay of *A Private War*?"

"It's not 'my' screenplay; it was written for Tradewind Productions. Therefore, it's their property," Lance answered mildly. "But I'm available tomorrow. I assume you want to talk about rewrites. How about you, Steve?"

"Of course. I cleared my calendar when Miss Sinclair said

she was coming to town," he said with a mocking salute in Jordan's direction. "How about tomorrow morning at ten?" He glanced around the table for affirmation. "All right. Ten it is then, my office."

Lance heaved an exaggerated sigh. "Now that we've got the business part of the evening settled, would you like to dance, Miss Sinclair?" he asked, motioning to the small dance floor that separated the dining room from the lounge.

"I don't thi—" She caught the devilish gleam in his eyes, daring her to step into his net. I'm not afraid of him, she told herself sternly. Besides, I'll have a chance to set him straight on the footsie-under-the-table bit. Levelly, she met his gaze. "I'd love to, Mr. Rutledge."

An almost imperceptible nod of his dark head acknowledged her decision before he pushed his chair back and rose. He held out a hand to her, and she accepted it, feeling strangely as if she were stepping out of her depth.

The pocket-size dance floor was crowded, and when Lance drew her into his arms, he held her closer than she liked. His arm curved against her back, pressing her into his hard body, and she could feel his warmth radiating through the sheer fabric of her dress. The spicy fragrance of his cologne as it blended with his own male scent was like a physical assault on her senses, and she realized that she was becoming more aware of this man than she liked or could afford.

She tilted her head back so that she could see his face. "Must you hold me so close?" she asked, wary of the unfamiliar sensations his touch evoked. "If I promise not to make a run for it, will you at least give me room to breathe?"

Brown eyes gleamed at her. "Haven't you noticed how crowded this dance floor is? I'm only trying to protect you."

"Is that anything like the wolf protecting the sheep?"

"Whatever can you mean?" he questioned innocently, laying his cheek against her hair.

She straightened away from the intimacy of the gesture. "That's what I mean. Also that footsie stuff under the table during dinner. You had no ri—"

"I beg your pardon," he cut in with mock severity. "I never touched your foot."

She felt like stamping her foot! "Foot! Knee! What difference does it make? You know perfectly well what I'm talking about."

"I can't help it if I have long legs and the waiter seated us at such a small table. They had to go somewhere."

Pulling her close again, he executed a flawless turn, and Jordan was surprised to find that they were now on the opposite side of the dance floor.

"Why did you do that?" Her voice reflected her suspicion.

"I like my body all in one piece." He grinned at her puzzled expression and explained, "Your friend, Collier, has been looking daggers through me ever since I asked you to dance."

She said nothing, recognizing the truth of his statement, and he laughed.

They drifted silently to a slow, sweet love song for a few moments, their bodies touching, both lost in their own thoughts. For Jordan, there was an uncomfortable, almost foreign, awareness of the lean, hard body pressed against hers. Emotions she had long thought dead were struggling to reawaken, and she tried to clamp down on them before they had a chance to bloom into life.

"Is there anything between you two?" Lance's drawl interrupted her musings.

Her mind suddenly blanked, and she was forced to question, "Who?"

"Collier, of course."

She leaned back against the support of his arm. "Why?"

"Because I need to know."

She couldn't suppress a smile. "And why do you need to know?"

"Because if there's anything serious between you, I'll be forced to put out a contract on him," he answered, deadpan. "If it's not serious, I'll let him live."

She laughed then, an easy, spontaneous sound that took them both by surprise. "Oh, let him live, by all means," she told him, sobering. "He's my agent. Nothing more, nothing less." Then, lest he mistake that admission for an invitation, she hastily added, "Not that it's any of your business."

"Of course it's my business." He touched his lips to the dark curls covering her ear. "I've decided everything about you is my business."

"I assume I have no say in this," she asked, trying to sound indignant.

"None," he agreed.

"Are you always this forward with women you've just met?"

"Only if they're as beautiful as you."

She had no comeback for that, and no time either. The song chose that moment to end and, with a look of genuine regret on his face, Lance dropped his arms and turned to escort her back to the table.

A quick glance at her watch confirmed what her body was telling her. She was tired, drained and, at that moment, wanted nothing more than to slip off her clothes and slip between the cool, crisp sheets of her bed. The thought made her quicken her steps, and she arrived at the table two steps ahead of Lance, ready to retrieve her evening bag and make her farewells.

Ryan, however, was again deep in conversation with Durrell, and Jordan wondered fleetingly what the two men, who had seemed such complete opposites, could find to talk about so earnestly.

"I hate to be a party pooper," she said to the small group, declining the chair Lance had automatically pulled out for her, "but I'm really exhausted. If you don't mind, I think I'll call it a night and go back to my room."

Audra Durrell was the first to answer. "Of course, you must be worn out. There's nothing more tiring than several hours on a plane and then having to suffer through boring business meetings."

Ryan and Durrell, roused from their discussion, scraped back their chairs. "I'll take you back to your room," Ryan offered.

"No, Ryan, please, stay and finish your drink and your conversation. There's no reason for you to end your evening because of me. Besides, my room's just a few floors down. I think I can manage to find my way alone."

"I'm ready to leave, too," Lance announced from behind her. "I'll be glad to escort Jordan to her room." Then he added when he saw Jordan stiffen, "On my way out, of course."

"That's not necessary," Jordan began.

"That would be great," Steven Durrell interjected, assuming the matter to be closed. "There are one or two more points I was hoping to discuss with Collier before tomorrow."

Jordan turned to Ryan in surprise, her eyes narrowed in suspicious questioning; but he met her gaze squarely, his own expression bland, before he stepped forward and kissed her cheek, saying quietly, "I'll call you for breakfast."

"Yes, fine," she answered, a little uncertainly, then leaned forward to say good-bye to Audra Durrell.

"It was all my pleasure," the young woman told her. "I hope we meet again someday."

"You seem to have made quite an impression on fair Audra," Lance murmured a few moments later as they made their way out of the restaurant.

Walking straight to the elevator, Jordan stabbed the down button. "She told me she'd always dreamed of being a writer."

"Admirable profession. Why doesn't she do something about it?"

She paced restlessly in front of the closed doors. "I asked

her the same thing. She said she didn't have the words to be a writer."

Lance laughed. "I guess they are a necessary commodity."

Jordan didn't answer, continuing her restless pacing instead. Lance Rutledge made her incredibly nervous.

She had already decided that Lance was a dangerous man; she was just now realizing how dangerous. She took another stab at the elevator button and tried her best to ignore him lounging negligently against the opposite wall. The trouble was that he was extremely difficult to ignore. He was a handsome, virile male, fully aware of the potency of his own charm.

"Punching the button isn't going to bring the elevator any sooner," he observed dryly, maintaining his careless pose.

Jordan sighed. "I guess you're right. I'm just not in the mood to stand here and wait for it. It's been a very long day." To add emphasis to her words, she raised her hand to rub the tight muscles at the back of her neck.

"I'm relieved to know it's not my charming presence that's making you tense."

Could he read minds, too?

His words had been spoken lightly, teasingly, but Jordan could sense a deeper undercurrent. She turned to look at him, still reclining casually against the corridor wall, the watchfulness of his eyes the only clue to the deceptiveness of his stance. Against her will and better judgment, she met his gaze and was unprepared for the range of emotions reflected there.

She was afraid she had understated the case when she had dubbed him dangerous. He was a threat to her peace of mind and her calm and ordered existence, an existence she had fought long years to achieve and maintain.

"Of course not," she lied. "Why should your charming presence, as you put it, make me tense?" She turned away from him. Those brown eyes saw too much, and she had already revealed enough of herself for one night.

"Oh, I don't know. Something about me is making you uncomfortable." He paused briefly. "Is it because I know about Rachel?"

His directness surprised her, and she turned back to face him. "I hope you're not going to persist in believing I'm Rachel. If you read the dust cover on the book, it plainly stated that *A Private War* was a work of fiction."

Lance lifted a dark brow. "Oh, I read it all right, but I'm also a firm believer in 'Don't judge a book by its cover.'"

The elevator doors slid open at that moment and a noisy group of partygoers, laughing, joking and more than a little drunk, spilled out into the foyer. A woman dressed in bright evening clothes sighted Lance and Jordan waiting to one side and exclaimed loudly, "Have you been waiting for the elevator long?" Her words were slurred. "We held it up. I'm sorry." She giggled helplessly. "But you see Harry, here"— she gestured to a man standing behind her—"he got his sleeve caught in the door, and we had to stop between floors. We thought we'd never get it loose."

She was still laughing as Lance and Jordan stepped through the sliding doors.

"Hilarious," Jordan muttered as soon as the doors closed.

An indulgent smile spread across Lance's tanned features. "Haven't you ever heard the old saying 'There's nothing worse than someone drunk when you're sober and—'"

"'Someone sober when you're drunk,'" she finished, pushing the button for the seventh floor. "Yes, I've heard it. Don't you ever run out of old sayings?"

He laughed. "I think I just did."

The elevator lurched into motion and Lance leaned against the back wall in what was now a familiar pose, while Jordan held herself rigidly straight, willing the elevator to reach its destination. She could feel Lance's eyes upon her but refused to turn and meet his gaze. He was too close, and tonight she was too vulnerable.

Her eyes followed the small light on the register above the door. She was enormously relieved when the elevator finally stopped at seven, and the doors slid open, allowing her to escape the close confines of the small car. She turned to say good-bye, certain that he'd be continuing on to ground level, only to find him standing beside her. He pushed her gently backwards through the opening just as the elevator doors slid together again.

For a moment she was too surprised to speak and he took advantage of the opportunity. "I'll walk you to your room. Which direction is it?"

"Thank you, but that's not necessary," she said when she found her voice. "It's late and I'm sure you're anxious to be on your way."

"In case you haven't noticed, my dear, this is the big city and lovely ladies like yourself should never be left on their own, especially at this time of night. What number are you in?"

"It seems you're always protecting me from something. It makes me wonder how I've managed all these years on my own."

"I've been wondering the same thing," he told her. "Now, which room are you in?"

"Lance, I've told you that it's not nec—"

"God, you're a stubborn woman!" He sighed heavily. "Look, I'm just going to walk you to your room. I'm not going to try to invite myself in, and I'm not going to make a heavy pass unless you want me to, so you've got nothing to worry about, do you?"

Good Lord, he could read minds! Exasperated, she shook her head. "I give up," she said finally. "Room seven-twelve."

"See how easy that was." His smile spread lazily across his tanned face. "Where is Collier's?"

"What difference does it make?"

"It could make a lot of difference," he drawled as they turned down the corridor to her room. "Especially if it's next door to yours."

She stopped and turned to face him. "I think you're

presuming quite a bit on first acquaintance, don't you, Lance?"

"Maybe." He lifted a hand to her dark hair. "But it doesn't feel as though we've just met. It feels as though I've known you for a long time."

He spoke quietly, yet Jordan could hear the sincerity in his voice. Afraid of the stronger emotion lurking just below the surface, she decided to go for the light touch. Her voice sounded slightly husky, even to her own ears, and she strove for a casualness she was far from feeling. "Is this a pass by any chance, Mr. Rutledge?" she asked lightly. "I distinctly remember hearing you promise not two minutes ago that there would be no heavy passes."

His smile came quickly and easily. "True, but this is a 'light' pass. They're allowed."

"Lance, I—"

"Shhh. Don't say it." His fingertips brushed lightly down her cheek. "You know I'd never do anything against your will, don't you? I'd never hurt you."

Something in his tone told her that he was again thinking of Rachel, and she felt oddly comforted, secure. Not that she'd let him know that, of course. "Could we cut out the light passes tonight so I can get to my room? I'm dead on my feet."

"Yes, ma'am. At your service, ma'am," he said in his un-California drawl as he pulled her arm through his and started down the hall again.

"You're not from California, are you?"

He lifted an eyebrow. "What gave me away?"

"Your accent. Or your drawl, to be precise. It's very similar to what I hear from native New Mexicans."

"You're close. Texas, born and bred."

"And proud of it," she guessed.

"And proud of it," he agreed.

They were getting close to her room and, perversely, she was sorry. "How did you end up in California writing movie

scripts?" she asked, aware that she was deliberately post-
poning the moment when they would have to part.

"I've always been a movie buff," he answered as they
stopped in front of her door. "When I was a kid, I used to sit
in the old movie house back home for hours watching Roy
Rogers and Gene Autry come riding across the screen over
and over and over. As I got older, I became more discrimi-
nating, thank goodness, but I never got over my fascination
with the movie world. While I was in college I wrote my first
screenplay and sent it to a well-known producer. He didn't
buy it, but he did write me a letter telling me that he thought
I had potential and that I should look him up when I
graduated. The Army interrupted my plans for a while, but
eventually I did and he offered me a job." His shoulders
lifted in a casual shrug. "The rest, as they say, is history. I've
been here ever since."

Curiosity overrode her normal caution. "Don't you miss
Texas? I mean, I assume you still have family there. Don't
you miss them?"

He shrugged. "Sure, some, I guess. But they've got their
lives and I've got mine. I go back and see them whenever I
can. My parents have even been out a few times to see me.
It's not as though I moved out of the country." He studied
her closely for a moment. "How about you? Do you ever
miss your home?"

Too late she realized how neatly she had walked into her
own trap. By questioning Lance about his home and family,
she had left the door open for him to do the same. Foolish,
Jordan, she chided, very foolish. What was it about Lance
Rutledge that made her forget herself for the first time in
eight years and break self-imposed rules never before
broken? Yesterday she would have sworn it couldn't happen. Tonight had proved that it could.

He was still watching her, waiting for her answer, and she
struggled for a neutral, if not quite casual, tone. "No, I can't
say that I miss it," she answered finally. "My family and I

were never very close even at the best of times, and when it came to the worst of times . . . well, let's just say they were as glad to see me go as I was to go."

He shook his head and lifted a hand to trace her jawline. "I can't imagine you doing anything bad enough to cause your own family to be glad you left." His eyes followed the path of his caressing fingers. "What did you do? Flunk algebra or get caught drinking moonshine? I know! You were caught in a compromising situation with the traveling shoe salesman. No? Well, then I just can't imagine. . . . Wait! I've got it." He snapped his fingers and brown eyes twinkled merrily down at her. "They found out you were a stripper at the Blue Light Lounge."

"Only on Wednesdays and Fridays." She couldn't hold back the laughter bubbling in her throat, and gave in to it, feeling her tensions ease with its release. "No, I'm afraid it's much worse than that," she told him, sobering a little. "I divorced their handpicked son-in-law."

He whistled softly. "Gee, that is bad. I can understand them turning out their own daughter after that."

"Yes, I suppose it was quite tactless of me," she said lightly, but the smile on her face slowly dissolved as she gazed up into the warm depths of Lance's eyes. Something was suddenly different. Even the air around her felt different. Gone was the casual, relaxed atmosphere she had been enjoying. In its place was a tension-charged sensation of expectancy.

As though mesmerized by the further darkening of Lance's eyes, she watched in silent fascination as his head dipped and his lips claimed hers in gentle, persuasive exploration. The kiss, tentative at first, slowly deepened as he tested her response, searched for resistance and found none. In truth, it never occurred to her to resist. She was too busy tasting, feeling, and experiencing.

At thirty years old, this was certainly not her first kiss. But where other kisses had brought with them a range of different reactions, from friendship and mild affection to fear and revulsion, nothing that had gone on before could have prepared her for Lance Rutledge. There was still an element of tenderness in his touch even as he took the kiss deeper. It was as though he instinctively sensed her needs, intuitively knew her wishes. She trembled as his tongue teased her lips apart, seeking and finding the dark sweetness within. Hands that had been tangled in her hair began a slow, rhythmic journey down her body, soothing and caressing first her shoulders, then her back, tighter at her waist, and threateningly close to her hips.

It was unlike anything she had ever known, and when they finally broke apart, she resurfaced slowly, her body swaying weakly against his. His hands at her waist held her steady as they clung to each other for the long moments it took to restore their breathing and heartbeats to near normal.

Pushing away from the intimate warmth of his chest, Jordan murmured weakly, "Just tell me one thing. Was that a light pass or a heavy pass?"

3

Her first thought the next morning was the same thought she had fallen asleep with the night before: Lance Rutledge. It was hard to decide which was more puzzling—his behavior or hers. On reflection, she decided hers won hands down. She sighed and stretched under the lightweight covers. Life was just full of little surprises.

That she had been so intensely attracted to a man was certainly a surprise. How had it happened? she wondered, desperately trying to rationalize her sudden interest in a member of the opposite sex after such a long dry spell. She had met many people over the last few years, some fascinating. But not one had drawn her the way Lance Rutledge had, even while common sense warned her to retreat.

She rolled to her side and glanced at the small travel clock beside the bed. It was almost seven. Ryan would be calling soon. She should get up and start getting ready, but a strange lethargy kept her still. This was an important day, she acknowledged. But equal parts of anticipation and dread immobilized her.

A small groan passed her lips as her thoughts returned to Lance. Why couldn't she get her mind off that arrogant, egotistical—no, that wasn't fair and she knew it. Lance had not tried to call attention to himself or his enviable status. Instead, he had repeatedly acknowledged her work and her merits as a writer, playing down his own accomplishments.

He was a flirt. She recognized that. But he was also warm and funny. And she sensed that, beneath the foolishness, there was depth that would surprise even his strongest critics.

But she had her own ghosts to lay to rest, her own battles to fight, and she didn't need the further complication of someone like Lance Rutledge in her life right now. Perhaps she never would, but especially not now. She had struggled eight long, painful years to get to this point. She couldn't afford the involvement that Lance wanted.

Then why couldn't she stop thinking about him? Why this utter fascination with the man? Why had she forgotten her own sacred, if unwritten, eleventh commandment?

The abrupt peal of the phone ringing jarred her from her reverie. She reached for the receiver, and after mumbling a hasty hello, she heard Ryan's clear tones and slumped back against the pillows.

"Don't tell me I woke you up," he teased.

Telltale traces of sleep lingered in her voice. "No, I'm awake, just not mobile."

"What you need is some fuel. How about breakfast?"

"Okay, but give me a little while to pull myself together. I don't think part of me knows I'm awake yet."

He chuckled. "All right, but make it snappy. I've got something I need to talk to you about and Durrell is sending his car for us at nine-thirty."

She sighed. Obviously she was about to find out what Ryan and Durrell had been so involved in discussing the night before. A sudden tightening of her stomach muscles warned her that she might not like it.

"Give me thirty minutes," she told him. "I'll meet you downstairs in the coffee shop."

"Good enough. I'll see you then."

Replacing the receiver, Jordan tossed back the sheet and slid regretfully from the warm comfort of the bed. Whatever this day held, she would have to face it sooner or later.

Ryan was already seated, a cup of coffee and the morning paper in front of him, when Jordan made her way into the coffee shop half an hour later. She smiled wryly when she noted that the paper was the *New York Times*.

"Really, Ryan, can't you leave New York behind for even a day or two?" she asked, sliding into a chair.

He glanced up from his reading, a sheepish smile crossing his smooth face for a moment. "You're early," he answered, folding the paper and laying it aside.

"Actually, I'm right on time," she corrected, "and you didn't answer my question."

He assumed a suitably serious expression. "I always like to keep informed. In my business, I can't afford to get out of touch."

She shook her head. "Poor Ryan. Don't you ever relax?"

"I didn't come here to relax. I came here on business. So did you," he added pointedly.

She smiled at that. "My, my. Aren't we subtle this morning?"

Ryan had the grace to look uncomfortable, but was saved from answering by the appearance of a full-figured young waitress bearing two menus and a pot of coffee.

After they had placed their orders and were once again alone at the table, Ryan took a quick sip of his coffee before replacing it on the saucer and pushing it aside. Reaching for Jordan's hand, he covered it with his own.

"I apologize for that, Jordan. I know I don't have the right to sit in judgment."

"No, you don't," she answered firmly, but softened her words with a smile. "Forget it. It's not that important. Besides, I thought you wanted to discuss something with me."

"As a matter of fact, I do." He leaned back in his chair. "Durrell made a very interesting proposal last night." He paused slightly. "He wants to buy the rights to *Paper Dolls.*"

Jordan realized that she had been expecting something along those lines. "I hope you told him it was out of the question."

If Ryan was surprised at her answer, he didn't show it. "No, it's a good offer. I told him I would discuss it with you."

She shook her head. "How can either of you think I would be interested after the fiasco with *A Private War?*"

"*Paper Dolls* would make a terrific film. I told you that the first time I read it. It might not be of the same quality as *A Private War,* but it has more mass appeal."

She stiffened. "And that's the name of the game? Mass appeal?" Her gaze narrowed. "I would like to know why Durrell is suddenly so interested in my books. Why am I being so honored?"

Ryan lifted a shoulder. "You're a good writer. Your books are very popular with a cross section of people, and they deal with timely subjects. What more could a producer ask for?"

"I think you missed your calling," she told him dryly. "I should have hired you as my press agent instead of my literary agent."

Ryan grinned but made no comment as the waitress arrived with their breakfasts. Over scrambled eggs and toast, he outlined the major points of Durrell's offer, and Jordan had to admit that it was interesting.

"Who would write the screenplay?" she asked in what she hoped were her most casual tones.

"Who do you want to write the screenplay?" Ryan countered, then shook his head. "Forget I said that."

"We both know that I know only one screenwriter, don't

we?" she asked tightly. "So I suppose I'm really asking if he would be the one to write the script."

"Durrell did say that if you agreed to the deal he was almost certain he could get Rutledge. He also said Jamie Masters is jumping at the chance to play Erica."

Jordan considered this latest tidbit as she slowly munched on her toast. Durrell was being more than a little presumptuous, already thinking about casting when she hadn't even agreed to sell the film rights yet, but she had to admit she was intrigued with the idea of Jamie Masters playing Erica.

Jamie was an up-and-coming young actress who was definitely superstar material. She had already earned high praise from some of the industry's toughest critics, and Jordan had to admit this put a new slant on Durrell's offer. From what Jordan had seen of her, Jamie Masters would make a perfect Erica. Even down to the physical description. And with Lance Rutledge writing the script, Jordan could definitely see the possibilities. . . .

"Why don't you take some time and think it over," Ryan suggested. "Durrell isn't expecting an answer today."

"That's good, since I have no intention of giving him one."

He leaned forward and Jordan could see the determination in his eyes. "Jordan, I don't want to influence your decision, and you know me well enough to know that I would never try to talk you into doing something you don't want to do, but I do believe Durrell's offer is worth consideration. I know you were disappointed in the way *A Private War* was handled, but *Paper Dolls* is a completely different type of story, much more straightforward, and I don't think there would be problems with it." He paused. "Also, I know you're not as close to it as you are to *A Private War*."

"And what's that supposed to mean?" she asked, her guard instantly rising.

"Just that," Ryan answered. "I know how strongly you feel about the subject, and I know how much time and research went into writing that story. I suppose it was inevitable that personally interviewing all those women would have an effect on you. At the time, I didn't realize how strong an effect."

Taking a sip of her now cold coffee, Jordan felt her body relaxing, her tension ebbing, her guard lowering. For an awful moment, she had been afraid that Ryan had guessed her secret too. But it seemed that only one man had the ability and the power to see inside her soul.

An image of Lance Rutledge flashed into her mind and she felt again a small tremor of excitement coursing down her spine. Why he affected her this way, she didn't know. How he had become the focus of her thoughts in such a short space of time, she didn't know either. But she did know that for the first time in eight years she felt attracted to a very male male, and more importantly, her desire to pursue this attraction almost outweighed her fear of it.

Then, as though from a distance, she realized that Ryan was speaking again and struggled from her daydream to follow what he was saying.

"—piece of cake for someone like Rutledge to write a snappy script. And with good casting"—he snapped his fingers—"you'd have a winner on your hands. Maybe not the dramatic success of *A Private War*, but a winner none-theless."

Her smile was tight. "I guess you're right. *Paper Dolls* is a lot of flash and glitter, but then it's a little more difficult to get deeply involved in the lives and loves of successful models than of women who are literally fighting for their lives."

"My point exactly," Ryan agreed. "At least consider Durrell's offer. I know you feel he botched *A Private War*, but *Paper Dolls* is more his type of story. Also, he wants this one badly. It could make a nice bargaining tool to insure that *A Private War* is produced the way you want it."

"All right," she conceded. "I promise to think about it, but I don't promise what my answer will be."

Ryan's smile was satisfied. "Fair enough."

Durrell's driver arrived at precisely nine-thirty and delivered them at Durrell's office exactly thirty minutes later. Jordan's palms were sweaty and her mouth dry as she stepped from the limousine, her nerves on edge for more than one reason. Her dread of the impending discussion—or battle, as she feared it might turn out to be—about *A Private War* was outweighed only by her reluctant anticipation of seeing Lance again. She hesitated a moment at the entrance but, catching Ryan's look of concern, she pinned a soft smile on her face and stepped forward into the luxurious confines of Steven Durrell's office.

Although she had heard no sound, and no outward actions betrayed them, Jordan had the immediate and uneasy impression that all was not well between Lance and Durrell. Durrell sat stiffly behind his desk, his expression tense, his face an unhealthy hue, while Lance appeared relaxed and at ease in a padded armchair to the right of Durrell's desk.

Both men rose to their feet as Jordan and Ryan entered the room. Durrell came forward, his hand extended, his professional smile in place, much as he had the night before at the restaurant. Jordan had not been fooled then; she wasn't fooled now. Durrell would be as polite and gracious as the situation called for him to be.

The usual polite greetings were exchanged, inane and meaningless, but expected. Jordan followed the ritual; she shook hands with Durrell and responded to his pleasant inquiries with courtesy. And all the while she was vividly aware that Lance had not once taken his eyes from her since she had walked into the room.

She turned to greet him, at once hesitant and expectant. She wanted to see him again, had thought of little else since he had left her at her door the night before. But now reluctance gave way to downright fear.

She desperately wanted to test her reactions of the previous night. Was there really an electric excitement between them? Did his eyes actually darken when he looked at her? Did she really feel more keenly alive in his presence than she ever had in her life? Or was her imagination running wild, her mind playing tricks with her?

No! Their eyes met, their gazes locked, and Jordan felt a tingling surge of warmth sweep down her spine and spread throughout her body. It was there. It was real. And it was most definitely wonderful.

Her smile transformed itself from perfunctory to promising. "Hello," she said softly.

He leaned toward her slightly, his gaze a gentle caress on her face. "Good morning," he returned. "I trust it is a good morning?"

"Yes," she responded, aware that there was a deeper, more subtle question being asked. "So far, so good."

He nodded, satisfied with her answer, and turned to shake hands with Ryan. He was dressed in well-cut slacks of dark brown that hugged his trim hips and emphasized the lean strength of his long legs. His shirt was pale yellow and of some soft material that clung to his broad shoulders and complemented the smooth bronze of his skin. And as hard as Jordan tried, she couldn't look away.

Durrell led them from his office down the hall to a large conference room. Lance fell into step beside her, but deliberately slowed his steps, putting more distance between them and the two men walking ahead.

"How long are you staying in California?" he asked, his voice low.

"I have a ten-thirty flight tomorrow morning. Why?"

"I was hoping to have some time with you after the meeting today." His smile was enticing. "Maybe do a little sightseeing, have dinner, take in a show. What do you think?"

"I don't know, Lance. I—" She caught the gleam of challenge in his eyes. "—All right, but on one condition."

His smile deepened. "Okay, let's have it."

"There will be no more 'light' passes like last night."

"Something told me that would be your condition," he drawled, his accent more pronounced. "All right, you have my word."

"Good, I'll look forward to it. I haven't seen very much of Los Angeles," she said, turning to face Ryan and Durrell, who were waiting for them by the conference room door.

"I'll make sure you see all the best parts," Lance promised, his voice soft, intimate.

He left her with no time to challenge him, but Jordan smiled as she promised herself he would find out soon enough that she wanted no repeats of last night.

Much to her surprise, the meeting went well. They made rapid and substantial progress, with Durrell conceding on several major points, points about which she had expected him to be unyielding. Perhaps Ryan was right, Jordan mused later when they had taken a short coffee break; perhaps Durrell did want *Paper Dolls* enough to compromise to get it. It seemed rather out of character for the producer, but then what did she really know about his character? This was only the third time she had met him and perhaps he had used his bullying tactics the day before in an attempt to intimidate her, to get his way without concessions.

Whatever the reasons behind his capitulation, she was grateful. She had not relished the idea of another clash, although she had no intentions of backing away from one. She had learned the hard way the importance of standing up for your beliefs, and if there was one thing in this world she believed in it was the story told in *A Private War*.

She was beginning to believe she had psyched herself up for nothing. An hour after the coffee break, they had gone completely through the script and Jordan was content with the result. She had won on all the major points.

Feeling relieved and satisfied, she leaned back in her chair, directed a smile in Ryan's direction and congratulated herself on her marvelous powers of persuasion, glad that the issue was settled and that she could get on with other things. She had a fascinating new plot working back in New Mexico and a very interesting evening ahead of her. All things considered, this had been an extremely productive trip and one she was glad she had made. Even Ryan, with his speeches on letting him take care of things, would have to admit that she had handled herself pretty darn well.

Then Durrell dropped his bomb and her moment of glory shattered around her.

"I'm very pleased with the results of our meeting today," he was saying. "As we all know, it takes a lot of hard work and determination to succeed." His gaze settled on Jordan. "I want to take this opportunity to thank Miss Sinclair for all her hard work and her 'determination.' Now that we've worked through the script, I can understand why you were so adamant about the way it should be written. I can only say that I was wrong and you were right and hope you'll forgive my ignorance."

Jordan was too stunned to react; the speech was so unexpected and so totally out of character that she could only sit in her chair, unguarded and unprepared for what was to come.

"We only have one more item to cover today before we adjourn this meeting," Durrell continued, his gaze now shifting around the room, "and that, of course, is the matter of the rewrite on the screenplay, or teleplay, if you will." He paused briefly, but significantly. "Lance informed me earlier this morning that he will not be available to do the rewrite . . . unless Miss Sinclair agrees to collaborate." Jordan's gasp echoed in the room, and Durrell raised his hands as in defense. "I've tried to talk him out of it, but he says those are his terms."

Silence reigned in the conference hall for several seconds before Jordan recovered enough to answer.

"But that's out of the question," she said shakily. "I've never written or even worked on a screenplay before. I would be useless. Besides, I have commitments of my own. I don't have time to take on another project."

"I agree," Ryan added to her protest. "I see no reason

why Jordan should have to involve herself in the mechanics of writing the script. We've resolved all the points in dispute. Every one is in agreement as to what the script should contain." He turned to Lance. "Why would you need Jordan?"

"The answer to that is very simple," Lance replied. "Jordan has final approval of the script. I, too, have other commitments. I'll be damned if I'm going to spend my time writing another script and have it rejected because something doesn't suit her." The look he gave her tempered his words. "I understand how important this project is to you, how important that it be handled properly. I believe this is the best way for all concerned. It will save time and errors."

"Impossible," Ryan exclaimed. "Jordan is facing a deadline on her current book, with another one only a few months later. She can't possibly take time out right now to work on this script." Anger drew his mouth into a thin line. "This wasn't part of the deal," he accused Durrell.

Durrell nodded. "True, but the deal changed somewhat when Miss Sinclair rejected the original screenplay."

"But this is ridiculous!" Ryan protested.

"You can always hire another writer," Lance suggested mildly.

"No!" Jordan cried out instinctively. She glanced around self-consciously before continuing in a softer tone. "I mean, we've come too far to risk everything now. Another writer might not understand." She knew she was handling this badly but made another attempt. "I mean, another writer probably wouldn't interpret the story the way we've worked it out today and that would mean starting all over again."

Durrell, ever the opportunist, seized the opening she had handed him and quickly said to Lance, "It shouldn't take very long to do the rewrite, should it? After all, it's not like writing the whole thing from scratch, is it?"

Jordan could feel Lance's gaze even though she refused to meet his eyes.

"No, it shouldn't take long. A few weeks at most," he answered.

Durrell looked at Jordan anxiously. "How does that sound to you, Miss Sinclair? Do you think you could spare a few weeks out of your schedule to work with Lance on the script?"

"That's not the question here," Ryan interjected.

"It's okay, Ryan," Jordan told him. "I'm far enough along on *Wind Chimes* that a few weeks isn't going to make that much difference." She turned to Lance, her face and voice void of expression. "When do you want to start on this?" She motioned toward the sheaf of papers stacked on the table. "Personally, I'd just as soon get it over with."

Lance studied her features long moments before answering. "I'm sorry, but I can't start right away. I'm in the middle of another project that will take at least three weeks to finish, and then I've got a couple of loose ends to tie up before I can start something else." He, too, kept his tone neutral, his face expressionless. "Why don't we say four weeks from Monday? That will be the first week of September. How does that fit into your schedule?"

"Fine, that'll be just fine." Pushing back her chair, she rose to her feet. With quick, jerky movements she began gathering up the notes and papers in front of her, preparing to stuff them into her briefcase. "I'll call you and let you know my flight and hotel arrangements."

Lance's next words forestalled her. "That won't be necessary. I was planning on coming to Ruidoso."

Her head snapped up. "Why would you want to do that?"

"We'll get more work done if I'm away from here and the telephone."

Her thoughts were chaotic, and it took a moment before she finally managed, "I don't think that's such a good idea. I can easily come here. I don't mind. It'll probably do me good to get away from New Mexico for a while."

"I was thinking the same thing about California," he

returned evenly. "Believe me, it'll be much better if I come to New Mexico. You wouldn't believe the interruptions I get."

She opened her mouth to protest, caught sight of the wicked gleam in his dark eyes, and closed it again. He was openly challenging her. *He thinks I'm afraid to meet him one on one,* she suddenly realized. *Well, I'm not afraid of him or his challenge. Since he's so interested, I'll be glad to show him the results of the last twelve years of my life.*

Transforming her frown into a soft smile, she heard herself sweetly concurring. "You're probably right. We would get more accomplished in New Mexico"—she paused slightly—"without all the interruptions."

His wide shoulders lifted slightly and one eyebrow arched inquiringly at her sudden acquiescence, but he said nothing. Jordan began gathering her things again, preparing to leave, and reached for her purse. She threw a quick glance in his direction at the same time.

He too was shuffling papers together. His head was bent and his sharply carved profile was all she could see of his face. But his expression was clear. He looked far from happy. *Well, too bad,* she thought bitterly. He had gotten what he wanted. Was he dissatisfied with his victory already?

Intuitively she knew that, with his uncanny perception, he would probably deduce the reasons behind her acceptance of his terms; and it made her uneasy that another human being, especially this one, had the power to read her thoughts and get inside her mind.

Ryan and Durrell were waiting silently by the door as Jordan picked up her things and walked toward them. She read disbelief and disapproval in Ryan's expression. He turned to Durrell as she neared the door.

"My flight back to New York leaves in less than two hours," he said tightly. "Could you ask your driver to drop me off at the hotel? I need to collect my luggage."

Durrell nodded. "I'll do better than that, I'll drive you

myself and take you on out to the airport. We can discuss a couple of things on the way."

Jordan stopped beside the two men. "Do you suppose I could cadge a lift to the hotel also?"

She felt the skin tingle on the back of her neck and knew that Lance had followed. Before Durrell could answer her request, she heard Lance's voice from right behind her.

"That's okay, Steve. You two can go ahead. I'll see that Jordan gets back to the hotel."

She opened her mouth to object, but Durrell said quickly, "All right, we'll be going then." He stepped out into the hall. "It was a pleasure meeting you, Jordan. I'm sure we'll meet again in the near future." He turned to Ryan. "Ready, Collier?"

"Yes, I'll be right with you," Ryan answered. He stepped toward Jordan, his gaze going over her shoulder to Lance. His expression was taut with displeasure. "Will you be all right?"

"She'll be fine," Lance answered for her.

Ryan ignored the other man, and leaned closer to her, his hand covering hers. "Call me when you get home. I think we need to talk." He kissed her briefly on the cheek. Then he too was gone and Jordan was left alone with Lance.

She rounded on him instantly. "You have got to be the rudest, most arrogant individual I've ever had the misfortune of meeting! If you think I'm going anywhere with you, my friend, you are sadly mistaken. I'm calling a cab to take me to the hotel and don't you dare try to stop me!"

He held up his hands in self-defense. "I wouldn't dream of it," he said, taking a step backwards.

"Good," she snapped, looking around the room. "Where's a phone?"

He pointed to a table in the corner and she stalked toward it, flinging her briefcase and handbag into a chair on the way. She grabbed the receiver and aimed a finger at the buttons before realizing she didn't know the number to call.

"What's the number for information?" she asked through tight lips.

"Four-one-one." His grin was wide and wicked, and it was all Jordan could do to keep from throwing the receiver at him. He was so smug, so unruffled, that his very stance was irritating.

She punched out the numbers and waited for the operator, quietly seething all the time. After obtaining the number for a taxi service, she got them on the line and, again, was forced to ask Lance for the address.

Lance supplied it, still in that agreeable, amused tone that further infuriated her. After repeating the address to the taxi dispatcher, she crashed the receiver back into its cradle and turned to face him, tense and ready.

He met her gaze levelly. "Would it be too much of an imposition for you to tell me what you're so upset about?"

"None at all," she flared quickly. "In fact, I'll be glad to." Hands on the table, she leaned forward. "The simple fact is, Mr. Rutledge, I do not like to be manipulated."

"Manipulated?" he repeated, his tone incredulous. "When have I tried to manipulate you?"

"When have you not?" she countered. "First, nothing will satisfy you but that we collaborate on the script, then you'll 'work better in New Mexico'"—her voice mimicked his—"and then I'm not even allowed to ride back to the hotel with whomever I choose. You don't call that manipulation?"

"I explained about the script and why it would be better if we worked at your place instead of mine." He sighed heavily. "I will admit that I thought working together might help us to get to know each other better, maybe even to become friends."

"Or something more than friends, perhaps," she suggested dryly.

His eyes were steady on hers. "That would be up to you, wouldn't it? Although I admit I wouldn't be averse to the idea."

"Well, you can forget it and you can forget about tonight too. I'm going back to the hotel. Alone."

"It doesn't have to be this way." He watched as she picked up her purse and briefcase and moved to the door. "I promised to be on my best behavior, didn't I?"

"And I'm supposed to trust you?"

"It would help," he answered in that amused tone she found so grating.

"Sorry," she answered briefly, her hand on the door.

"Heartless, aren't you?"

She almost smiled at that, but caught herself just in time. Didn't he take anything seriously? A moment later, he answered her unspoken question.

"Jordan, I never meant to manipulate you," he said softly. "But I do want to get to know you better and I want you to get to know me. Is that so bad?" His voice dropped to a husky whisper. "Can you honestly say that you don't want the same thing? Is it wrong for two people who are attracted to each other to pursue it?"

She recognized the compelling, seductive quality of his words and fought against the desire that welled within her. Why did this man have to be so attractive? But even as she wondered, she realized that Lance's physical characteristics were not the power behind the pull. There was something else, some quality, some distinction in him that she had not encountered before.

Drat the man! Why couldn't he have been sixty years old, fat and balding? Instead he was tall, lean and devastating. Exactly what she didn't need in her life right now.

She felt her anger ebbing, cooling as quickly as it had flared. With Lance's charming blend of sincerity and humor, she was finding it difficult to stay mad at him for long. But looking at him now, seeing the mischievous gleam sparkling from the depths of his dark eyes and the wide grin he made no effort to hide, she decided that anger was probably her best defense.

"Would you please quit looking at me like that," she

snapped, turning away from him. "You look like an over-grown cocker spaniel."

He laughed at that. "Does that mean you've reconsidered?"

"No, it means I'm still going back to my hotel . . . alone."

He shrugged. "I'm crushed, of course, but just to show you what a gentleman I am, I'll walk you out front. Your taxi should be here by now."

Astonished by his abrupt capitulation, she could do little but follow him down the hall, through the wide reception area and out to the front steps. She didn't understand why his giving into her wishes disappointed her so; she only knew that she suddenly felt alone and strangely abandoned.

Her taxi was indeed waiting for her when they reached the front entrance. The driver was leisurely reading a newspaper, his feet propped comfortably on the front dash. Lance leaned forward and opened the back door for her; the driver only grunted as he laid his newspaper aside and straightened in his seat.

"Where to?" he threw lazily over his shoulder, and Jordan grimaced at the lackadaisical manner of the man.

Lance supplied the name and address of her hotel, and the driver nodded knowingly, making a great show of turning on the ignition and starting the meter. Lance's grin was devilish as he closed her door and waved good-bye with a mocking salute. As the cab turned out into the street, Jordan could see him loping easily toward the side of the building and the parking lot beyond.

The driver was obviously in no hurry as the cab slowly made its way through the Saturday afternoon traffic. He made no attempts at conversation, for which Jordan was immensely thankful. She had no desire for small talk; her thoughts were too disturbed and chaotic for polite chatter.

Outside the taxi, the scenery of L.A. passed as a large blur, with Jordan minimally aware of her surroundings.

Inside the taxi, she was seriously contemplating giving into a strong desire to scream, anything to relieve her mounting frustration. She refused to think about the inconsistency of her feelings.

She leaned back against the cracked upholstery of the aging vehicle and closed her eyes against the bright California sunlight streaming in through the windows. Fatigue washed over her, and she slumped deeper into the seat, the thought of her cool, comfortable room at the hotel silently beckoning like an oasis in the desert.

She had run the complete gamut of emotions today, she acknowledged wearily, from excitement and anticipation to satisfaction and a sense of accomplishment to disappointment and disillusionment, the latter emotion being no one's fault but her own. She had broken her own cardinal rule, but luckily the reckoning had come early, before too much damage had been done. And to think she had believed herself immune. What a joke! When would she ever learn?

But Lance seemed so different. For eight years she had lived by her own gut feelings, and they had never steered her wrong. Not until now, she amended. Her gut feeling said that Lance Rutledge was a different cut of man, but just look how he had—

She was so deep in her thoughts that it took a moment for her to realize someone was speaking to her. "Uh, I don't mean to disturb you, lady," the driver said apologetically, "but do you know anybody that drives a fancy little sports car, maybe a Ferrari? Whoever it is has been on our tail since we hit the expressway."

"Why, no," she answered, turning in her seat to peer out the grimy back window. "I don't even know anyone in Los Angeles. . . ."

A feeling very close to jubilation rushed through her even before she spotted the cream-colored sports car. Her earlier exhaustion melted away, and when she turned back around in her seat, a soft smile of satisfaction curved her lips. So she hadn't been wrong after all, she thought joyously, glancing again over her shoulder at the small car following closely behind. And although the sun reflected brightly off the small car's windshield, she knew only one person could be driving that vehicle. She'd never admit it, but he had just made her day.

Her smile widened as she met the driver's puzzled gaze in the rearview mirror. "It's okay," she told him. "It's just a friend of mine. I was expecting him."

4

Lance eased his foot from the car's accelerator. The taxi driver was obviously in no hurry. The twenty-minute trip from the studio to Jordan's hotel had already stretched into thirty, and his patience was beginning to wear thin.

His mouth crooked into a wry grin as he thought with anticipation of his next meeting with the cab's passenger. The grin broadened as he remembered the scene at Durrell's office. But his delight faded as he considered her anger. The last thing he wanted was to put further distance between them. He'd been intrigued by the author; he was fascinated with the woman.

Jordan Tyler Sinclair. An unusual name for an unusual woman, he thought. The memory of her face drifted through his mind like a familiar song and he felt the same stirrings of desire as when he'd first seen her.

He had told the truth when he'd said she wasn't what he was expecting. After reading *A Private War*, he'd been prepared to meet someone older, more world-wise, perhaps even a little scarred around the edges. It was hard to imagine that anyone could live through the kind of hell she obviously had and not show it. But instead, he'd found her soft and young and beautiful. He remembered how her body had felt when he'd held her in his arms the night before. He could still taste the sweetness of her mouth and feel the smoothness of her skin under his hand. There were no visible scars, but, he reminded himself, there were scars other than the physical kind and he knew Jordan had more than her share.

He knew about scars. He had several of his own. A few were the consequence of an impulsive childhood and a stubborn will. Others were the result of leaping first and looking later. The deepest and most painful was the after-effect of his own marriage and divorce. He could sympathize with Jordan. That scar healed most slowly.

He thought about the script he'd written for Durrell. He had expected her to hate it, but it wasn't until he'd met her that he had realized how bad the script really was. He wouldn't have blamed her if she'd taken it as a personal insult. Durrell's version couldn't have been further off the mark. Jordan was quick and bright and sensitive, totally unlike the character he'd created on paper. With no effort on her part, she was able to arouse feelings and emotions in him he'd have sworn were dead and gone.

Not that there hadn't been other women in his life. He grimaced at the thought. There had been an almost constant parade of women through his life since Stephanie. And since he'd won the Oscar . . . well, it was amazing what a hunk of gold-plating standing on your mantel could do for your social life.

No, the feelings and emotions Jordan aroused were different, not that he'd try to deny his obvious desire for her. He shifted uncomfortably in his seat at the thought of it. But she also made him think of his Southern upbringing and all those lectures from his parents on the proper way to escort a lady. She brought to mind long walks and country lanes, holding hands and stolen kisses, and tenderness . . . a tenderness one normally associated with motherhood and newborn children.

His hands clenched on the steering wheel. How had that crept into his thoughts?

A picture of Stephanie as he'd last seen her flashed into his mind, and his body tensed with familiar anger and bitterness. Years had not diminished his hate or disillusionment. Betrayal was a hard crime to forgive. Disgust welled in the back of his throat and he tried to banish the disturbing thoughts from his mind.

But some thoughts were hard to push aside, and the image of Jordan holding a round-cheeked infant with its mother's dark hair and deep blue eyes could not be denied.

He watched the taillights of the taxi ahead as it slowed and prepared to turn into the hotel entrance. Impatience surged through him again, and he considered getting out and giving the cab a push. Was the driver doing this just to irritate him?

Lance whipped the Ferrari around the taxi as soon as it cleared the driveway, and pulled into the parking lot. Sliding into the first vacant slot he saw, he quickly stepped out into the bright California sunshine. Today, he decided, was a very good day to get on with the rest of his life.

Jordan mentally squared her shoulders as the taxi rolled to a stop in front of her hotel. A uniformed doorman hurried forward to open her door and she stepped from the car. She tried to ignore the tension building at the base of her neck as she made her way up the steps to the hotel lobby. She hesitated at the doors, then turned to wait for Lance to join her.

Alternate flashes of irritation and excitement coursed through her. She'd never had this much trouble convincing anyone she didn't want his company before. On the other hand, when had just the mere sight of that "anyone" made her knees weak and her insides quiver?

She watched as Lance sauntered across the parking lot toward her. She tried not to concentrate on his tall, lean frame or to notice the way his muscles rippled under the silky material of his shirt. She refused to let her eyes linger at the vee of his throat where his shirt was unbuttoned, revealing the first curlings of dark hair, and she tried her best to ignore the flexing of the muscles in his thighs as he walked.

She didn't want to acknowledge the accelerated pounding of her heart or give in to the smile that tugged at the corners of her lips in response to his. She wanted to hold on to her anger, her self-defense, but she felt it slipping further away the closer he came.

She squared her shoulders and prepared herself for round number two with Lance Rutledge.

He stopped at the foot of the steps. "Jordan—"

Coolly, she interrupted. "Why did you follow me?"

"I wanted to see you, of course."

Oh, of course. How silly of me, she silently mocked, but the quick thrill of pleasure his words brought denied the mockery in her thoughts. "I told you I was coming back alone."

He nodded. "I know, and you did." His grin held the hint of deviltry she was coming to know so well. "Being the gentleman that I am, I would never interfere with a lady's plans."

"Then what, may I ask, are you doing here?"

He held up a hand. "You only said you wanted to come back here alone. You didn't say what you were going to do once you got here. Besides, as I remember, we have a date this afternoon."

"And as I remember, I told you the date was off." She turned and walked to the hotel door. "It was nice seeing you again, Mr. Rutledge."

Ignoring her words, he followed her through the glass entrance. "You'll probably want to change clothes before we go. It gets pretty airy with the top down." He eyed her linen suit and strappy heels. "Did you bring any jeans or slacks with you? You'll need some comfortable shoes, too. Sightseeing's no fun if your feet hurt."

She stopped walking. "Are you deaf?"

He took her arm and urged her toward the elevators. "I must not be if I can hear you ask. Come on, it's almost two o'clock. The day'll be gone before we know it."

Still she hung back. "I almost feel sorry for you. Do you always have this much trouble getting a date?"

He grinned but continued to pull her along. "No, believe it or not, you're the first I've had to coerce in a long time."

She watched him push the call button for the elevator with fatalistic acceptance; he obviously wasn't going to accept her refusal. She didn't know whether to be annoyed or relieved.

The elevator doors swished open before she could decide. She stepped inside and took quick note of the dark carpet and somber walls. It was only recently that she'd noticed how small elevator cars really were.

And in such close confines, it was impossible not to be aware—and God, was she aware!—of her fellow passenger. Unnerved, she tried to rationalize her reaction. Eight years was a long time to repress normal physical desires, she reasoned calmly, and Lance Rutledge was an attractive, personable man capable of arousing these . . . these physical desires in any normal, warm-blooded female. Why should she be any different? Now that she knew where the danger lay, surely she could avoid stepping on the mine.

"Jordan?" His voice was a warm caress and she jumped guiltily, fervently praying that this time he couldn't read her mind.

"Lance, I—" She cleared her throat and tried again. "I . . . what if I told you I really don't want to go with you this afternoon?"

"Do you really not want to go with me this afternoon?"

Her mind searched feverishly for an answer. She opened her mouth but no sound emerged. She moved her lips, but her tongue felt dry and thick. Her throat ached with suppressed emotion.

The lurching halt of the elevator couldn't have been more welcome. She stepped quickly, blindly, into the corridor and almost turned in the wrong direction. His touch was gentle on her arm as he guided her down the hallway.

Outside her room, she fumbled with the door key. He watched her for a moment before removing the key from her shaky fingers and unlocking the door. He handed her the key and she tried to smile her appreciation, but her lips were stiff and rubbery, and she feared that their movement appeared more like a grimace. She stepped into the room, then turned abruptly to face him.

"Lance, I—"

His hands on her shoulders propelled her backwards. "You're always saying that. Go change, Jordan, and relax." He crossed to the French doors that opened onto her small balcony. "I'll be a gentleman, again, and wait out here for you."

She watched him step outside, then sighed in frustration. She just couldn't get through to him. Couldn't? a voice inside her head asked, or was it that she really didn't want to? She turned away from the thought, but the voice persisted. Wasn't it easier to accept her attraction to a man if she didn't have to take responsibility for it? Look what he made me do, she could say later.

A moan of despair started in the back of her throat. When had she become such a coward? Years ago she had taken full responsibility for her life and its direction. Could she, in good conscience, relinquish that responsibility now?

She walked to the mirror over the dresser and stared at her reflection. If she went with Lance today, she would have to acknowledge that it was her decision and be able to accept the consequences of doing so. She could no longer pretend that she had no choice in the matter. Other women dated—even the word sent a tremor through her body—surely she could do the same. After all, nothing could happen that she didn't want to happen . . . could it? Taking all her rather shaky confidence and determination in hand, she marched to the closet and flung open the door.

A few minutes later, dressed in tailored slacks and a cool blouse, she stepped out onto the balcony. She was still nervous, but tried to convince herself that her anxiety was justified. After all, how many years had it been since she'd been on a date? How long since she'd tolerated the presence of a man in her life?

Lance's back was to the door and she cleared her throat to gain his attention. He turned to face her, approval and appreciation lighting his dark eyes.

"I'm ready."

"So I see."

"Shouldn't we go?"

"We should, but I don't think I want to."

She blushed, but refused to be intimidated. "I think we'd better."

His smile held genuine regret. "I think you're right. I could get in a lot of trouble if we hang around here." He gestured to the door behind her. "Shall we?"

They were in the elevator, headed back down to the lobby, before she thought to ask, "Where are we going?"

"It's up to you. Where would you like to go? Is there anything special you'd like to see?"

She gave the question some thought. "I've always wanted to visit Beverly Hills and see how the stars live, and Rodeo Drive; I've heard a lot about Rodeo Drive. Then there's the beach; I've never been to a beach. And—" Her voice trailed off when she saw the laughter in his face.

"Anything else?"

His grin was infectious and she had to smile with him. "I sound like a real tourist, don't I?"

"That's okay," he said, taking her arm and escorting her through the lobby. "Some of my favorite people are tourists."

Bright, hot sunshine greeted them as they left the hotel and Lance directed her to his car. She eyed the Ferrari warily. Its low, sleek frame fairly screamed of speed and the thrill of the race.

"This thing isn't going to get me killed, is it?" she questioned Lance across the hood.

He looked offended. "Who, Betsy? She's as gentle as a baby." He gave the car an affectionate pat. "You'll think you're riding in a station wagon."

He opened the door for her and she slid down into the padded comfort of the seat. She watched as he folded his long legs into the compact interior. A moment later the engine throbbed to life and Jordan was greeted by a quick rush of wind as the car pulled out onto the roadway. Her hair streamed behind her and she put up a hand to try and control it.

Lance laughed at her struggles. "I told you it was a bit airy with the top down." He turned his gaze to the traffic. "What kind of car do you drive?"

She lifted her voice to be heard above the wind. "I have a Jeep."

If she'd intended to surprise him, she'd succeeded. He looked at her blankly. "A Jeep?" he repeated.

She laughed at his expression. "Yeah, you know, a Jeep. Four-wheel drive, canvas or hard top, roll bar—"

"I know what a Jeep is," he interrupted. "I just can't picture you driving one."

"I live in the mountains, remember?" She tried to shield her eyes against the brightness of the sun. "We get a lot of snow and ice, not to mention wind and rainstorms. I'm not fond of being stranded, so I bought a Jeep."

"You actually live in the mountains?" His gaze took in her tailored clothes and leather sandals. "Forgive me for pointing out the obvious, but you don't exactly look like a mountain dweller."

She rummaged through her purse for her sunglasses. "Mountain dweller is not necessarily synonymous with hillbilly, you know. But, yes, I actually live in the mountains." She found her glasses and slid them on her nose. "My house is about six miles out of town and sits on the side of a hill overlooking a small valley. There's a creek and a pond, if you want to call it that, and lots and lots of pine trees."

"Sounds impressive. I'm anxious to see it."

Nerves tightened the muscles in her stomach. "Lance, I want to talk to you about that." Seeing the question in his eyes, she hurried on, not giving him a chance to interrupt. "I know you said it would be better if you came to Ruidoso, but there's no need for you to come all that way. I'm sure you can handle the script without my—"

He broke into her monologue. "You know, your dedication just amazes me. How you can sit there and calmly discuss business when you're starving is beyond me."

She blinked her confusion. "Am I starving?"

"Of course you are. I'm surprised you hadn't noticed."

"Lance, we need to talk. This is important."

"I know, I know," he soothed in a gentle voice. "But I promise I'm a much better guide when I'm not faint with hunger."

The restaurant Lance chose was small and homey, its darkened interior a welcome relief from the bright sunlight outdoors. That he was well known there became immediately obvious. He was greeted by name by everyone in the place and directed to the best table in the house. Menus were quickly thrust into their hands and Jordan couldn't help but notice the effusive manner of the young waitress hovering over them.

"I eat here often," Lance explained when they were at last alone. Then, noting the direction of Jordan's gaze, he commented, "Mona wants to be an actress."

"Oh, Mona does, does she?" She smiled at the waitress's retreating figure. "I would never have guessed."

"There are lots of aspiring young Monas in this city." A wry smile touched his lips. "Long on talent; short on luck. I guess, in a way, I identify with them. It hasn't been that long since I was young and eager to show my stuff."

Jordan found this glimpse into his past fascinating. "Was it difficult? Breaking into the business, I mean?"

His brows drew together. "I was luckier than most, I suppose. I had an in when I came here—not that there weren't several lean years at the beginning while I tried to prove myself."

She tried to imagine Lance as a struggling, impoverished young writer, but the image of the man as she saw him now was too vivid to be replaced. The strength, the self-assurance, the casual acceptance of his own worth were too natural to be simulated.

She shook her head. "I can't imagine you as an underling," she told him.

He laughed at her description. "Ah, but I was. And for more years than I like to remember. I started out as a staff writer for a production company. My first jobs were mostly in television, cowriting sitcoms, specials, whatever was on the agenda at the time. It was a long time before I got a chance to work on anything big enough to really make a name for myself."

"And yet you stuck with it?" she asked as the waitress set their plates before them.

"Oh, I stuck all right." He picked up his fork. "My biggest problem was that I felt stuck. There were many times when I considered chucking it all and going home."

She eyed her plate solemnly. "Why didn't you?"

He glanced up at her. "Go home?" She nodded. "Lots of reasons: pride, determination, stubbornness. Any or all of the above. When I left home I was the local boy going to Hollywood to make good. I couldn't go home with my tail tucked between my legs. Besides, I was doing what I wanted to do. I wanted to be a writer. I figured if I could hang in long enough my chance would come."

"You were obviously right."

"Oh, obviously," he answered with a self-deprecating grin. "What about you? How'd you end up a writer?"

Warning bells sounded immediately. She toyed with her meal as she sought a safe answer. He'd already read her life story; how could she answer without giving more of herself away?

She finally opted for a half-truth. "Nothing exciting, I'm afraid. There didn't seem to be anything else I was suited for."

"I find that hard to believe." He gave her an easy smile. "I'll bet you're a lady of many talents."

She laughed, but heard the bitter edge in her voice. "They must be hidden talents, then. I've never found them."

Lance studied her face over the rim of his glass. He, too, had caught the bitter edge of her tone but, given what he knew of her past, he was not surprised at its presence. He wanted to ask her about that past, to learn everything he could about this woman, this enigma who sat beside him, but he held his tongue, aware that it wouldn't take much to lose her completely.

He decided on a casual approach. "Ah, Jordan. You're a modest woman. You have so many talents, you're not even aware of them all."

She arched a skeptical brow. "Such as?"

"Of course I don't know you all that well, yet"—he stressed the last word—"but I've already seen a few examples. From my own experience, I know you're a great dancer. Good timing, poise. Ginger Rogers should be so graceful."

She laughed but motioned for him to continue. "Don't stop now. I'm beginning to enjoy this."

"Then there's your skill at negotiation. I've never seen Durrell handled any better."

She shot him a dry look. "I noticed it worked well with you, too."

"And you're diplomatic. Diplomacy is a real talent. Many people go for years and never master diplomacy, but you've already got it down pat."

She almost choked on her laughter, but he ignored her

and continued, motioning with his fork. "Look at that outfit you're wearing. You obviously have a great talent for fashion. And let's not forget your real biggie—kissing! What a—"

"Enough, enough!" she interrupted, but couldn't keep the smile from her voice. "I should have known better than to turn a Texan loose. They never know when to quit."

He watched the blush fade slowly from her cheeks and thought again how lovely she was and, surprisingly, how vulnerable. No one could blame her if she'd turned hard and cold. He'd even expected it.

"You're originally from Denver, aren't you," he asked a moment later. His need to know her was so strong that he decided to take a chance. "Is your family still there?"

He saw the guard instantly rise.

"Yes." She kept her voice carefully neutral. "They still live there. Greenwood Village, actually."

"They must be very proud of your literary success."

A light flashed in her eyes for a moment before it was carefully extinguished. "Yes, I suppose they are. We've never discussed it."

Her answer did not satisfy him, but it told him a lot. He looked down at his plate. "Do you visit them often?"

She glanced at him sharply. "Not too often," she answered, and he could hear the anxiety in her voice. She pushed aside her half-eaten lunch and looked down at her watch. "Hadn't we better be going?" she asked with determination. "It's after three, and I still haven't seen Los Angeles."

He recognized her ploy for what it was but knew he couldn't ignore the distress he saw in her eyes. There were so many other questions he wanted to ask, but he had seen her withdrawal and knew that now was not the time.

Jordan couldn't wait to get back to the car and sit down. She was hot and tired and her feet were sore. She couldn't remember the last time she'd walked so far. Lance had certainly taken her seriously when she said she'd like to go window-shopping on Rodeo Drive.

"Some shopper you turned out to be," he said after they'd settled into the car. "And after all that, you didn't buy a thing."

She lifted her hair from the back of her neck. The sun was settling lower in the western sky but its heat had not subsided. "That's what window-shopping's all about, Lance. Besides, who could afford to buy anything there? That one little scarf"—she measured with her hands—"hardly long enough to go around my neck and they wanted eighty dollars for it. Hmmph!"

He laughed as he fit the key into the ignition. "Welcome to California, Jordan. Now you know why they call it the Golden State."

He eased the car smoothly into the late afternoon traffic and they rode in silence for several minutes. Jordan rested her head against the seat and let the wind ripple through her hair. She stretched her tired legs and wiggled her hot toes, content to watch the city sliding by until Lance turned onto the coast highway.

She straightened in her seat and looked around. "Where are we going?"

"The beach, fair lady." He tossed her a lopsided grin, then continued in his best tour-guide voice. "We've seen the mansions and swimming pools of Beverly Hills and window-shopped on Rodeo Drive. The next stop on our guided tour is the popular California beach at Malibu."

"Sounds wonderful, but is there someplace along the way we could stop for a cold drink? I'm as dry as a bone."

The look he gave her was properly lecherous. "Have I told you how much I like your bones?" He waggled his brows at her. "But yes, I know just the place. Not only can we get something cold to drink, but if you're nice to the owner, we might also get something to eat."

Suspicion reared its ugly head. "Do I, by any chance, know this 'owner'?" she asked, unable to mask her apprehension.

His hand covered hers and he gave it a gentle squeeze before turning his attention back to the highway. "Trust me, okay? That's all I ask, Jordan. Just trust me."

Just trust me. The words chased themselves around in Jordan's head. Just trust me. So easy to say, but so hard to do. Just trust me.

She raised her hand to push her hair from her eyes and was not surprised to find that it was shaking. Just trust me. Just put yourself in my hands. He had no idea what he was asking.

A casual date in the middle of the day was one thing. She stared at the sun sinking further into the west. Going to a man's home, alone and at night, was quite another. Especially a man she'd just met. One she knew practically nothing about. Good God, she didn't even know where she was going. And no transportation . . . she couldn't even leave when she wanted to.

Her panic was obvious as she clutched at his sleeve. "No, Lance, I can't. Let's go back. I can't go to your house. Please take me back to the hotel. Please, Lance."

The sound of tears was in her voice and Lance quickly pulled to the side of the road. Her body was trembling as he gathered her to him. He cursed his own stupidity. He knew her fears. He'd seen her vulnerability. But in his haste to draw her into his world, he'd ignored every sign and warning.

He held her away so that he could see her face. "I'm sorry, Jordan. I didn't mean to rush you." His voice was husky, deepened by emotion. "Don't be upset. I'll take you back."

She stared into the clouded darkness of his eyes, too bemused by what she saw there to answer. There was no doubt about the sincerity of his apology. Her husband had never felt the need to apologize to her, no matter what the offense. For Jordan, it was a novel experience.

Slowly, her body ceased its trembling. "Lance, why did you want me to go home with you?" She watched him for his reaction. She wanted to see the deceit for herself if it was there.

He met and held her gaze. He didn't blink, he didn't flinch, he didn't waver. "You wanted to see the beach; I have a house at Malibu. It overlooks the ocean. You wanted a cold drink and someplace cool and relaxing. I have a large supply of ice and I never turn off the air-conditioner." Finally, he did lower his eyes, but brought them back to hers almost immediately. "Jordan, I'd be lying if I said I wasn't attracted to you. I am and I have been since I first saw you. I took one look at you and knew I was hooked. I think you're bright and beautiful, smart and sexy, just about everything I'd want in a woman. You're easy to talk to, fun to be with, you've got great legs"—he paused—"and I can't think of anything I'd rather do than spend the whole night making love to you. But I won't. That's what I want you to understand. It wouldn't mean anything unless you wanted it too. And, regretfully, at this moment, you don't."

She opened her mouth to speak, but he held up a hand. "You don't have to explain. I understand better than you think I do. I know you're not ready. We've just met." His shoulders lifted in a rueful shrug. "Is it my fault my libido works faster than yours?"

She had to smile at his candor, but still was not allowed to speak. His finger against her lips silenced her. His touch was gentle and her lips trembled. As though mesmerized, he watched the movements of his finger as it traced, then retraced, the curved fullness of her lips. Then Lance seemed to shake himself from the trance, and he removed his hand to let it rest on the wheel.

"I guess what I'm trying to say is that it's your ball game, at least for now. You call the shots, you make the rules, and

I'll follow, at least as long as I can. I don't know how to be any more fair than that." He hesitated for a moment before taking a deep breath and charging ahead. "I can't promise not to want you, or touch you, but I do promise that you can trust me. I'd never do anything against your will. If that's not enough, Jordan, I don't know what else to offer you."

He held his breath for a long moment before she answered.

"You remember that I asked you for something cold to drink?" She watched his face as he nodded. "Well, I think I'm hungry too. What have you got to feed me?"

5

∞∞∞∞∞∞∞∞∞∞

The view from Lance's deck was spectacular. Deeply, she breathed in the tangy sea air and laughed in delight when she tasted salt on her lips and tongue. The sun's final rays spread a golden glow across the rolling water, and Jordan's eyes feasted on the beauty of the Pacific at sunset.

The tide was out. Fascinated, Jordan watched the gentle lapping of the waves as they washed onto shore in a seductive rush of surf and spray. Her toes curled against the leather of her sandals, and she fought against the urge to kick them aside. At the moment, she could think of nothing more satisfying than running barefoot across the sand, feeling its wet, gritty texture cake the soles of her feet and squish between her toes.

It must be wonderful to live by the ocean, she mused, watching foam and water splinter against low-lying rocks just beyond the shoreline. She loved living in the mountains, but she acknowledged that, even in their towering majesty, they could not compete with the wild freedom and primitive beauty that rolled before her.

A glass door slid open behind her and she turned to see Lance, a tall glass in each hand, step out onto the wooden deck.

"Here you are," he said, handing her a glass. "Something tall and cool, just as you requested."

She looked at the amber contents, then to the lemon, lime and orange wedges decorating the rim. "Is this something I can handle?"

He smiled at her hesitation. "I think so, unless you're allergic to iced tea."

She shook her head and took a deep swallow of the cold liquid, enjoying the tingling sensation it created as it slid down her throat.

"Oh, that's great." She took another sip and smiled at him. "You have such a way with tea bags."

"It's all in the wrists," he said, flexing one to demonstrate. "Would you like to sit down?" He gestured to one of several lounges and deck chairs scattered around them.

"No, thanks. Your view has me hypnotized." She turned her gaze back to the roiling ocean. "I'm afraid if I stop watching, it won't be there when I look back."

He nodded in understanding. "I know. I felt the same way the first time I saw it. In fact, it's one of the main things that sold me on this place. I came to look mostly out of curiosity. I was sure it was out of my price range and probably bigger than I needed. But it had belonged to an actor and his wife. The marriage had gone bust, so had his career, and he wanted to unload. One look and I was sold."

"I don't blame you. It's a marvelous place." She sighed with pleasure. "I'll tell you a secret if you promise not to laugh."

He crossed his heart in solemn ritual.

"I've never been to the ocean before, but I think I'm in love already. It's so beautiful . . . and so breathtaking . . . so—I can think of a hundred adjectives and none of them seems to fit. Awesome, maybe that's the word I'm looking for."

He chuckled at her enthusiasm. "Would you like a closer look?"

"Could we?"

"Of course. I know the owner."

He led the way from the deck down wooden steps to a narrow grass ledge.

She looked around her in amazement. "Is this all there is to your backyard?"

He halted before a stone staircase that led to the beach. "No," he said, swinging his arm in a wide arc. "That's my backyard."

"Some backyard." She nodded her approval. "I thought I was going to get a closer look."

"Right this way." He motioned to the stairway, then looked pointedly at her sandals. "You'd better leave those here. Sand can be hell on the footwear."

She dropped to the grass without hesitation and began pulling off her shoes and rolling up her pant legs. She glanced up to find him watching her, smiling.

"Shouldn't you take yours off, too?"

His brows rose in a comical leer. "Now that's a proposition if I ever heard one."

That remark earned him a punch in the knee, and he dropped down beside Jordan clutching his leg in feigned agony.

"Now see what you've done. I'm injured."

She threw him an aggrieved look. "Careful. You're beginning to look like a cocker spaniel again. Besides, you deserved it."

His grin was positively wicked as he leaned toward her. "Does this mean you don't want to kiss it and make it better?"

"You catch on fast for a country boy." She pushed him backwards and sprang lightly to her feet. "Come on, slowpoke. I want to see the beach while it's still light enough to see it."

"Spoilsport," he grumbled, but rose to follow.

The moment her feet touched the warm powdery sand, Jordan was enraptured. Before her stretched mile after endless mile of shimmering ocean and unbroken horizon. In them she saw the same characteristics that had drawn her to the mountains: unbridled freedom.

Jordan valued freedom above all else in this world; it was the true treasure of life. Perhaps it was because she had paid such a high price for her own independence that it meant so much to her. Perhaps it was because she had lived for twenty-two years without it—eighteen years under her father's thumb, four more under Philip's. How could anyone take all this for granted?

She ran to the ocean's edge. Deliciously cool water lapped gently at her bare feet, and she had an almost irresistible urge to fling her arms open wide in a gesture of greeting and welcome. She smiled at her own temerity. How could anyone embrace an ocean?

She spun around, seeking Lance, and almost lost her balance. He was right behind her. He reached out to steady her. Their eyes met, but his gaze seemed to go below the surface, into her mind. She wondered what he saw. With anyone else, she would have resented the intrusion. With Lance, she merely accepted it as natural. He was a strange man, an unpredictable man, she decided, but in an odd way, a comforting man.

The thought surprised her, stunned her. Was she losing her mind? How could she possibly think of Lance as comforting? Wasn't this the same man who had murmured, thirty minutes after meeting her, "who could know more about Rachel, than Rachel?"

He was getting too close. She knew it, but she felt powerless to prevent it. Something about him drew her. She was like a moth drawn to a burning candle, but her fascination with the flame overruled her fear of the fire.

Warm fingers stroked her cheek, bringing her back to the present. "What are you thinking about?"

"About you," she answered, choosing the truth, and saw

surprise in his expression. "I was thinking what a nice man
you are." His eyes narrowed at that. "How different you are
from most men." She paused again. "And how much I like
your backyard."

His fingers traced her jawline. "In that exact order?"

It took an effort to hold her pulse steady. "Is the order
important?"

"You'd be surprised."

He took her hand and began walking along the closely
packed sand of the shoreline. Jordan pulled him to the
water's edge, letting the surf suck and swirl around their
ankles. The sun was sinking lower against the western
horizon, shedding its last rays against the churning water.
She watched in fascination.

"I can't believe it's so beautiful."

Errant breezes lifted her long hair and tossed it around her
face. With gentle fingers, Lance brushed the dark hair from
her cheek. "Neither can I," he told her, but he wasn't
looking at the ocean.

She felt the familiar flutter in her stomach and attempted
to step away from him. His hold on her hand prevented her.
"You're good for me, Jordan. You make me appreciate what
I'd begun to take for granted."

"You should never take this"—she motioned to the scene
surrounding them—"for granted. It's too special. You're
very lucky to have it."

"Yes," he agreed. "But I'm finding of late there are things
more important."

She was grateful for the failing light that hid the color
touching her cheeks. "Lance, I hope you don't get the
wrong idea about my being here today. I—"

He cut her off. "Come on, it's getting dark. I'd better go
fire up the grill if I'm going to feed you."

He slipped an arm around her shoulders and led her back
toward the stone staircase. She was midway to the top
before his voice stopped her.

"I was right about one thing, though," he told her.

"Oh? What's that?" She turned to look down at him.
"You do have fantastic legs."

Jordan wandered aimlessly around the large living room,
trying to get to know Lance, leisurely examining things that
were a part of his everyday life. She strayed to the stereo
and flipped idly through his record albums, noting their
similar tastes in music. A grouping of abstract paintings
caught her eye, and she studied them for a moment trying to
understand what the artists had meant to convey. She failed
and moved on, going from object to object, picking up a
whatnot, reading titles from his bookshelf, endeavoring to
absorb the personality of the man who lived there.

In the center of the mantel, stood the golden statuette, the
Oscar. Best Screenplay. She couldn't begrudge his pride in
his achievement. No one could. She only wished her script
had turned out so well the first time.

But that wasn't necessarily true, was it?

She turned away from the mantel. If it had been written to
her satisfaction the first time, she wouldn't have come to
California to contest it, and she wouldn't have met Lance
Rutledge. Although part of her argued that it would have
been for the best if she hadn't, another part of her could not
deny the pleasure meeting him had brought.

Was she opening herself up for heartache? Only time
would tell, she decided, and she was going to try her best not
to worry about it. There was time enough for that when he
came to Ruidoso and they had to work together on a
day-to-day basis.

His voice called to her from the doorway. "Are you any
good in the kitchen?"

She walked toward him. "A little. Do you need some
help?"

"Anytime I'm in the kitchen, I need help." He led her to a
sunny room at the back of the house. "I'm not exactly
efficient at this sort of thing. I thought you might fix a salad
while I put these steaks on the grill."

"I think I can handle that," she told him, glancing around at the beautifully coordinated kitchen. If Lance didn't use this room, someone else certainly did. Copper-bottom pots hung over a center work island, a built-in rack held utensils and cutlery, and every kitchen appliance known to modern woman lined the counter top. A ceiling-to-floor window looked out over the deck, but its ocean view was obscured by hanging plants and a cactus terrarium.

"Looks like someone enjoys the kitchen." She nodded to the plants in the window. "Yours?" The words were out before she could stop them.

"Heavens, no." He laughed and turned back to the meat he was seasoning. "This is Ina's domain. I can't grow weeds, much less those things." When Jordan didn't answer, he turned to look at her. "Ina Talmadge is my housekeeper. Unfortunately, she's off on weekends or you could have met her. She's a sweet, sweet lady who takes excellent care of me." He paused and smiled. "She's also old enough to be my grandmother."

That's it, Jordan, she told herself, disgusted. Stick your foot in it. Why was it everytime she opened her mouth around the man, she made a fool of herself? She'd never noticed that particular defect before, and hoped it wasn't the start of a new trend.

She pushed her hair from her face. "Lance, I'm sorry. I didn't mean to pry. It's just that I don't normally . . . I guess I'm just not used to . . . what I'm trying to say is that I don't—"

"—make a practice of going to a man's home, especially one you haven't known very long." He took her hands and pulled her close. "It's okay. You don't have to say it. I'm very flattered that you made an exception in my case, but what I said in the car still goes." He tightened his fingers around hers. "There is no other woman. I would never have brought you here if I were involved with someone else."

She dropped her gaze to the tile floor between them. "It's none of my business, Lance. I feel like a fool putting you in a position where you feel obligated to explain. It seems I never say the right thing around you. Do you know if hoof-and-mouth disease is terminal?"

"Idiot," he chided gently. "I didn't feel obligated. I wanted to explain." He tilted her chin up until their eyes met. "You shouldn't feel foolish. You're a very cautious lady. I respect that."

She wanted to thank him—for what, she wasn't sure—but the words caught in her throat. The past twenty-four hours had played havoc with her emotions and she felt very open, very vulnerable.

Uncomfortable, she pulled her hands free and walked to the counter. "If you'll show me where everything is, I'll get started on that salad."

He grinned, pleased that he could unnerve her. "Vegetables are on the cutting board behind you. Bowls are in the cabinet to your left. I think you can find everything else." He picked up the platter of meat. "I'll be outside on the deck if you need me."

She waited until he left the room, then released the breath she'd been holding. Turning back to the counter, she picked up the vegetables, carried them to the sink and dumped them in.

Lance watched her through the windows. Behind him, he could hear the hiss and sizzle of the meat on the grill, but his mind was not on cooking. His thoughts surged and flowed around the woman. He'd never seen a more beautiful sight than Jordan Sinclair chopping vegetables in his kitchen, her feet bare, her dark hair falling past her shoulders in tumbled disarray. Her movements were graceful and controlled, unlike the jumpy, jerky motions he sometimes witnessed when she was with him.

Clearly, he made her nervous, but the thought did not displease him. It was a beginning. And certainly better than indifference. He'd have to work harder for affection.

He turned his attention back to the grill as the back door slid open and she stepped out onto the deck.

"All through," she said, smiling. "How are the steaks coming?"

"See for yourself," he invited. "How do you like yours?"

"Medium rare." She watched the fire suddenly blaze. "When I have a choice."

He gave her an offended look that made her smile again. "Your faith is overwhelming." He held one up for inspection. "See? A perfect medium well." He looked closer. "If you don't count the edges."

Jordan laughed and shook her head at him. "Didn't I say that's just how I like it?"

"It's a good thing." He looked at the shriveled piece of meat again. "Come on. We'd better eat this thing before it gets worse."

They decided to eat in the dining room. The lights were dimmer, Lance explained, and with him as cook, who wanted to see what they were eating?

The steaks were not as bad as he'd predicted. Then again, she could have been eating sawdust biscuits for all the difference it would have made. Sitting beside Lance, his knee—again!—touching hers under the table, who could worry about such a mundane matter as food? Tonight, it was enough just to be close to him, caressed by his gaze, entertained by his voice. He told her ridiculous little stories about Hollywood personalities he had worked with. He told her that when his big break came along, he almost didn't recognize it.

"True, it was a feature film," he said, taking his third helping of salad. "But have you ever heard the term 'a sleeper'? This one was more like 'in a coma.' It was so bad, I was ashamed to have my name on the credits. Are you going to eat the rest of your potato?" He helped himself from her plate, but continued talking. "You can imagine how surprised we all were when it hit big at the box office. We'd been thinking of it as a big joke, but the next thing we knew, it was an overnight sensation. I've been working steadily ever since."

"I know. I've seen your work and I approve."

"I've read your work. I also approve."

"Thank you. Do you think we qualify for the 'mutual admiration society' yet?"

"I think we just passed the entrance exam."

She toyed with her water glass. "I was glad you won the Oscar. I thought you deserved it." I was also very disappointed that you weren't there to accept it in person, she could have added. I watched the whole show hoping to get to see you. "We'd just started negotiations with Durrell when your nomination was announced. I had already seen *All the Long Days* and I was very impressed when he mentioned you as the screenwriter."

"And very disappointed when you saw the screenplay."

She glanced down at her plate and felt tension starting to build at the base of her neck again. "You might say that. At first, I didn't believe you had written it."

"Considering how awful the script is, I'll take that as a compliment."

"I might as well tell you," she said in a confidential tone. "I was very nervous about meeting you."

"I don't know if I should be flattered or offended."

"Both, probably." She saw his puzzled look. "I was excited about meeting Lance Rutledge, the Oscar winner. But I was mad as hell at Lance Rutledge, the screenwriter— even more so when you didn't show up at that meeting in Durrell's office yesterday."

The look he gave her was appealing. "I didn't know about the meeting or I'd have been there. I wanted to meet you, too. You're quite a celebrity in your own right."

She shook her head, and he watched the long, dark curls slide around her shoulders.

"I certainly don't feel like a celebrity." She pushed back her chair and began stacking dishes. "We'd better get these done. I've got to get back to my hotel soon."

"Leave them," he told her and laid his hands over hers. "I'll see to them later."

Reluctantly, she straightened away from the table. "Are you sure? It wouldn't take but a minute—"

"I'm sure. Besides, there's something I want to show you."

He took her arm and steered her to the outside deck again. The sound of the surf was louder now, the incoming tide intensifying the pounding beat. Even the breeze was stronger. The moist tang of sea and salt was more pronounced. It whipped at her hair, tangling the dark strands around her face and neck. Lance reached out to smooth it away, and Jordan felt time stop, suspended for a brief moment, as their gazes locked and their minds touched.

The sudden shift in atmosphere almost overwhelmed her. It had been the same the night before. One minute they were having a casual conversation, and the next, the air was charged with electricity. Awareness of herself, of Lance, even her surroundings was heightened, sharpened, for that brief span of time. It was as though her senses had been brought into sharper focus, and she could suddenly see more clearly, hear more clearly, even feel more clearly.

She was surprised when he dropped his hand and stepped away from her. She told herself that she was relieved, that she was far from ready for a big seduction scene, but she felt a sense of loss when he walked to the railing.

"The only thing more beautiful than the Pacific at sunset," he said, his gaze on some distant point, "is the Pacific in moonlight." He held out his hand to her. "Come look at my backyard now."

She hesitated only a moment before accepting his hand and stepping beside him. He was right about the view; it was magnificent. Moonlight transformed the sandy beach into a ribbon of shimmering silver, and its reflection on the rolling water was like an iridescent flame, dancing across the surface.

"I don't know how you ever leave here." She tilted her

head back and gazed up at the starry sky. "I'm surprised you're not a hermit. How long have you lived here?"

"Last month was three years."

"That's the same time I moved into my house," she said, amazed at the coincidence.

"What made you decide to move to the mountains?"

She considered that for a moment before she answered. How do you explain freedom, privacy, escape and solitude?

She said instead, "A change of scenery, mostly. How about you? How did a swinging bachelor end up in a secluded beach house in Malibu? Or is the question redundant?"

He laughed. "It's been a long time since I thought of myself as a swinging bachelor. But I guess I chose this place for much the same reason you moved to the mountains. I needed a change. I was tired of apartment living. Tired of nosy neighbors." He leaned his back against the railing and folded his arms across his chest. Wind whipped his hair into charming disorder. "My closest neighbor was a mother-and-daughter acting team. The mother was forever after me to write a script for her daughter or help find her an acting role. The daughter couldn't act for beans and was homely besides. At the time, this place was very appealing."

"I can see why." She turned her gaze to the house. "One good thing about this place, it should be big enough if you ever decide to raise a family." God, the moonlight must be getting to her. She couldn't believe she'd said that.

She brought her eyes back to his and found him studying her. The expression on his face was one she had never seen.

"I've been married before," he said in a voice she didn't recognize.

That fact shouldn't have surprised her, yet it did. Some faceless, nameless woman shouldn't have disturbed her, yet she did. Jordan thought of the beautifully decorated rooms inside the house. "Did she . . . I mean, did the two of you live here?"

"No, we were divorced a long time before I bought this place."

"What happened?" She told herself she wouldn't ask, but the words were out before she could stop them.

"We found we weren't going in the same direction." That was one way of putting it, he reflected bitterly. He couldn't bring himself to tell the whole truth. He doubted if Jordan would want to hear about Stephanie's abortion. "You know how it is," he said, and saw Jordan flinch under his words. "Two people start out on the same road, wanting the same things, dreaming the same dreams. Then something comes along and one veers off. They're just not on the same road anymore."

A bitter laugh almost escaped her. Had she and Philip ever been on the same road? If they had, she couldn't remember it. They'd always walked on Philip's road, thought Philip's thoughts and dreamed Philip's dreams. What she'd wanted had never mattered.

His voice snapped her back to the present. "You've been married before. You should understand what I'm talking about."

"Oh, yes. I understand." She was only partially successful at masking her contempt.

"How long were you married?"

"Four years," she answered stiffly. "You?"

"Three." A brief hesitation. "Any children?"

A tight ball of misery knotted her stomach. "No, no children."

"What happened? Why did you divorce?"

"Lance, I'd rather not talk about this, if you don't mind. It's ancient history, anyway. Why is this so important to you?"

"Because you're important to me." He laid his hands on her shoulders. Her skin was cold under his fingers. "Because I want to know you, know everything about you. I'm very close to falling in love with you. I don't want to make the same mistakes he made."

"Lance, please. Don't say that. We just met. You can't possibly—"

"Love you? I assure you it is very possible. I've never been so attracted to a woman in my life. Not even my wife."

"But it's wrong. I'm all wrong. Can't you see that?"

He tried to pull her closer, but she held her body stiff. "Why is it wrong, Jordan? Why can't I love you? Why can't I get close to you?"

She whirled away from him, going to stand at the top of the staircase, her unseeing gaze fastened on the restless rhythm of the surf. Love. How could he talk about love? Why was he doing this?

She felt his presence behind her. "Lance, I'm not ready." She swallowed the constriction in her throat. "I'm not ready to get involved with anyone."

"Why, Jordan?" He took her shoulders and turned her to face him. "You said you weren't Rachel. You said it wasn't your story. What happened to make you feel this way?"

"Please. I don't want to talk about it. It's not something I like to remember." She shivered.

Lance measured her with narrowed eyes. "*A Private War* is your story, isn't it?"

"No!" She brushed away from him impatiently. "No. How many times do I have to tell you that? It wouldn't be anything to you if it were."

"You're wrong, Jordan. Have you already forgotten?"

She looked at him blankly. "Forgotten?"

"Last night. I told you I was making everything about you my business."

She wanted to stomp her foot in exasperation. "Let's just cool this for a while, shall we? The whole thing is getting way out of hand. I think my attraction for you is the fact that you think I'm Rachel, and therefore, feel sorry for me." She drew herself up to her full height. "Well, believe me, I don't need that kind of affection."

Lance's chuckle startled her. "I don't feel sorry for you,"

he told her. "If I feel sorry for anyone, it's me. I'm the one who's going to have to put up with you."

She treated him to an icy glare. "No one's asking you to put up with anything. Now if you're through with your chuckle, perhaps you'll be good enough to take me back to my hotel."

She attempted to brush by him and return to the house, but his hand on her arm prevented it. "Running won't help, you know. There's an old Hollywood line, 'This thing's bigger than both of us,' and in our case, it's true. I can't stop my feelings for you any more than I can stop the tide from coming in." Lance studied her face. "If you're honest, Jordan, you'll admit that you've felt it, too. It may sound like a cliché, but I think we were meant to meet—meant to be together. Besides"—a grin teased the corners of his mouth —"I'm a hell of a catch. You couldn't do any better. Don't you read the gossip columns?"

She almost laughed then, but decided she wasn't ready to give up her anger or forgive him. He'd had no right poking and prying, making her remember things she struggled every day to put behind her. She certainly didn't need a meddlesome man in her life, even one as appealing and attractive as Lance Rutledge.

"At the risk of losing the world's most eligible bachelor, I'd still like to get back to my hotel room. It's late and I'm too tired to argue properly with you."

"Too tired, huh? If your resistance is low, maybe I should keep you here and persuade you to my way of thinking."

She cocked her head and looked him up and down. "My resistance is never that low."

He winced. "Was that nice? I think I'd better get you back to your hotel. Your claws are beginning to show. I knew you had them; I just didn't know when you'd unsheath them."

The drive back to town was accomplished in near-silence. They were each involved in their own thoughts, and small talk seemed unnecessary. When they pulled up to the hotel entrance, Jordan hoped to say a quick good-bye and make a hasty retreat, but Lance insisted on escorting her to her room, admonishing her about the dangers of the big city.

"Have you already forgotten what I told you last night?" he asked, as he pressed the elevator button for her floor.

"I can't believe that every woman in L.A. has a personal bodyguard," she retorted.

"True, but you should read the headlines sometime. Do you want to be a statistic?"

"Why do I argue with you?" she murmured. "You never let me win."

When they reached her door, he took the key from her suddenly nerveless fingers and slipped it into the lock. He pushed the door open, but did not attempt to accompany her inside.

He pressed her key back into her palm and curled her fingers over it. "Here you are, fair lady. Safe and sound. Don't you feel better?"

"Yes, thank you. And thank you for a lovely day. I enjoyed seeing Los Angeles."

"The pleasure was mine."

She shifted nervously. "Well, I guess this is good-bye."

"Not good-bye," he corrected. "Until we meet again." He took her hands in his and pulled her closer. "Your memory is really terrible tonight. Have you forgotten September?"

"No, I hadn't forgotten, but I hoped you had."

His hand lifted to her cheek and he traced it lightly with his thumb. "You're asking the impossible." His hand slipped to the back of her neck and pulled her closer. "Beautiful Jordan," he murmured an instant before his lips crushed down on hers.

Gone was the tentative, patient exploration she remembered from the night before. This kiss was hungry and demanding, and he gave her no time to resist. He sought her response and, willing or unwilling, she gave it.

His arm hooked around her waist and pulled her closer,

while his other hand, tangled in the dark thickness of her hair, cupped her head and held it immobile. His lips moved over hers in fierce possession; her lips parted. Her soft breasts yielded against his hard chest, and she struggled to hold on to her sanity. This urgency was new to her. This need, hot and overwhelming, made her dizzy. Where had it come from?

Then, as suddenly as it had come, the storm subsided. The tempo changed, slowed, calmed. Lance's lips eased their pressure, until they moved against hers in teasing softness. Gently, his mouth touched and tasted, sipped and nibbled. He rained soft, light, butterfly kisses over her face, her nose, her eyelids, coming back to her lips to trace their shape, test their flavor.

She drew away from him but rested her head against his shoulder. Her breath returned in trembling shudders. "You confuse me, Lance Rutledge. Is that your plan? To keep me off-balance?"

He tipped her head back so that he could see her face, then leaned his forehead against hers. "I told you we were fated. Do you still not believe me?"

He was so close she couldn't think. Their breaths mingled as they stared at each other. A sudden spark in Lance's eyes warned her of what was to come, but even as she opened her mouth to protest, his head was lowering once more toward hers.

"Sshh," he whispered softly. "This has to last me a month."

After only a heartbeat of hesitation, she lifted her lips to his, consciously welcoming the embrace. His mouth closed over hers, and he parted her lips hungrily, seeking the sweetness that was within. His tongue was a sweet aggressor, stroking, teasing, probing. She moaned and clutched at his shoulders, returning pressure for pressure, taste for taste, sensation for sensation until, finally, she drew back from him, flushed, trembling and shaken.

He watched her struggle for composure and smiled in

satisfaction. "Something to remember me by when you get back to Ruidoso." Bending close, he dropped another quick, hard kiss on her lips. Then, stepping quickly away, he lifted his hand in a mocking salute.

"You've got a month, sweet Jordan. Just a month. I'll see you in September."

6

~~~~~~~~~~~~~~~~

I'll see you in September.

His words played through her mind again as Jordan studied her kitchen calendar. Sunday, September 1. He'll be here tomorrow.

She moved to the counter to pour a cup of coffee, then left it standing as she prowled restlessly around the room. She had been jumpy and irritable all morning and was even more annoyed when she'd finally forced herself to acknowledge the source.

Lance Rutledge hadn't been out of her thoughts for more than a few hours at a time since she'd left California. But then whose fault was that, she reminded herself. He was constantly doing something to make sure that she thought of him. There were phone calls at odd hours of the day and night, greeting cards with nonsensical sayings, and notes with silly poems. One had contained a beautiful poem about love and promises. She'd almost cried when she read it.

If his intention was to remain prominent in her thoughts,

he was succeeding admirably. When she tried to concentrate on her work, she heard his voice. When she tried to relax, read a book, or even sleep, she saw his face.

How had she allowed this to happen? she asked herself for the nine hundred and ninety-ninth time. How could she have lost control of the situation so completely? But the answer, she feared, would not be flattering. One look at Lance Rutledge and her will had turned to putty.

For the umpteenth time, her memory replayed the scene outside her hotel room. Every detail was indelibly imprinted upon her mind, and her face flamed in remembrance. Could that really have been her, welcoming his embrace, returning his kisses? Could that have been her, yielding to his temptation, responding with such abandon when just the thought of another man touching her left her cold, even disgusted? Could that have been her own body, suddenly turned traitor?

She dropped into one of the kitchen chairs, cradling her head in her hands. If he was able to affect her like this after only one weekend, what could he accomplish in the time it took to rewrite the script?

A light tapping interrupted her musings, and she turned to see her closest neighbor and dearest friend peek around the back door.

"Are you working?" Monica Corbett asked.

"No, I'm brooding," Jordan answered. "Come on in and cheer me up."

Monica opened the door wider and a small bundle of energy with red gold curls hurled itself across the room to be caught up in Jordan's waiting arms. She hugged the baby and kissed her dimpled cheeks and chubby chin. She was rewarded with a smacking kiss in return.

Monica watched them from the doorway. "Good grief, you two. You act as though you haven't seen each other in a month instead of just a few hours."

Jordan tickled the soft skin at the baby's nape until she giggled. "Mommy's just jealous, isn't she, Angie?"

"Ha! That'll be the day. After this morning, you're welcome to her."

"Uh oh, it sounds as though you're in trouble, little one." Jordan smoothed the child's rumpled curls. "What did you do to make mommy so unhappy?"

"She woke me up at this ungodly hour, that's what. Look at that." Monica pointed to a wall clock over the table. "It's not even nine o'clock yet."

Jordan smiled at the lovely redhead as she lounged against the counter. "Maybe you shouldn't stay out so late at night, then nine o'clock wouldn't seem so ungodly."

Monica waved her arm in a gesture of dismissal. "No lectures please. What I need is some caffeine. Got any coffee cooking?"

"There's a fresh pot right behind you."

Monica, familiar with Jordan's kitchen, crossed to the coffeepot and helped herself. Her brows arched when she saw Jordan's full cup, cooling on the kitchen counter, and commented over her shoulder, "I see you've got all your wheels rolling this morning, too." She indicated the cold coffee. "Want a fresh cup?"

Jordan frowned. "Might as well. I forgot I poured that last one. Maybe a shot of caffeine will get me going, too."

Monica carried the cups to the table, placing Jordan's out of Angie's reach, then slid into the chair across from her. She tried to hide a yawn behind her hand.

"I assume from the silly look you were wearing last night when you came in that you had a good time." Although she'd played baby-sitter the night before, by the time Monica had come in, Jordan had been too tired and sleepy to ask any questions.

"You might say that." Monica's smile was wistful. "Glenn is such a nice guy. We had dinner at that new place out on the highway. You know the one you and I talked about trying."

"Did you like it?" Jordan asked, as she tried to control Angie's squirming movements.

"Mmmm, very much. I could get used to living the good life."

"Oh, you could, could you?" Jordan laughed at her friend's dreamy expression. "I guess you lead a hard life now?"

"You know what I mean. Good wine, good food, dancing until dawn. Well, maybe not dawn, but—"

"I'd say three in the morning was close enough to dawn."

Angie decided that she had sat quietly long enough. Jordan let her wiggle her way to the floor, then watched as she headed to the toy box standing in the corner. When Jordan turned back to Monica, she was surprised to see a blush staining Monica's cheeks.

"You didn't dance until three, did you?" she probed gently.

Monica shook her head. "No, we went to his place for a nightcap."

"Oh, Monica. Do you think that was wise? You've only known Glenn for a couple of weeks."

"Nothing happened," Monica told her curtly. "We just talked and got to know each other."

"But still," Jordan persisted, "going to a man's home, especially at that time of night."

Abruptly, Monica rose and walked to the coffeepot. "Good grief, don't make a federal case out of it. I told you nothing happened. We just talked. Besides, I know him better than you know Lance Rutledge, and you went to his home."

Jordan stiffened at the reminder. "You're absolutely right, of course, and I didn't mean to sound critical. It's none of my business how you spent your evening."

Monica was immediately contrite. "Oh, Jordan, I'm sorry. I didn't mean that the way it sounded."

"That's okay. I guess you just hit a sore spot." Her eyes shifted to the calendar. "I told you I was brooding."

Monica followed Jordan's gaze, her eyes widening with comprehension. "Tomorrow's the big day, isn't it?"

Jordan nodded. "I'm afraid so. That last note he sent said he'd be here on the second."

"Oh, I'm so anxious to meet him. He sounds wonderful."

"Pardon me if I don't share the same sentiment." That wasn't quite true. "Right now I think the whole thing is nothing but a nuisance."

Monica looked horrified. "You don't mean that."

"Yes, I do. I don't know why I ever agreed to any of this. I don't know anything about writing a screenplay."

"You said Lance offered to teach you everything you needed to know. Besides, I think it would be exciting to work on a movie, especially one from your own book. Just think of it; your name will be on the credits, you might even be nominated for an Oscar."

"An Emmy, Monica. This is a television movie, remember?" Jordan said dryly.

"All right. An Emmy, then. There's nothing wrong with that. I would think you'd be excited about it. This might open up a whole new career for you."

"I don't want a new career. I have enough trouble with the one I have. I'm behind schedule on *Wind Chimes* and don't have a single idea for the second book on my current contract." She stared into her empty cup. "The last thing I need right now is Lance Rutledge underfoot."

Monica moaned beneath her breath. "I don't understand you, Jordan. A man like Lance only comes along once in a lifetime, and that's only if you're really lucky. For most of us, he never comes along at all. And this one likes you. For God's sake, don't blow it!"

Jordan turned away and busied herself at the counter. "Don't you think you're overstating the case a bit, Monica?"

"No, I don't!" she answered forcefully. "But I do think if someone doesn't give you a push in the right direction, you'll stay an ostrich forever."

Jordan spun back to stare at her. "An ostrich!"

"Yes, an ostrich. You know the big chicken who sticks her head in the sand every time she feels a little threatened."

Monica sighed and closed her eyes. When she spoke again her voice was quiet, constrained. "Jordan, you're probably not going to like what I'm about to say, but you're my best friend and I think this needs saying. I don't believe it's the script that has you worried. You're a good writer, and you're adaptable; you've proven that more than once. I believe you can handle the script just fine. I think the reason you're spooked is Lance Rutledge. And I think what scares you is Lance the man, not Lance the writer."

"Don't be ridiculous, I'm not scared of Lance," Jordan protested. "I just don't have time for another project right now. I explained that to you."

"Smoke screen," Monica said succinctly.

"I don't believe I'm hearing this. You, of all people, know me better than that. I run my own life; I don't live behind fear."

Monica rose to stand beside her. "Yes, you do, Jordan. You fear the future because of your past. You fear the past because of the pain you still live with. But in this case, I think your biggest fear is of yourself."

"Now you are being ridiculous. Are you saying that I don't trust myself to be around Lance?"

Monica shrugged. "If the shoe fits."

Jordan studied her friend in amazement. "What in the world gave you that idea?"

"Several things," Monica answered. "One was the way you floated around here on a cloud after you got back from California, but denied that Lance was the cause for it. Another was all the cards and notes and poems he sent you. You tried to act so blasé about them, but I could tell you were pleased, even a little excited."

"Am I so transparent?"

"Just to me, and that's only because I know you so well."

Jordan shook her head and turned to the kitchen window, staring out at the mountain scenery with unseeing eyes. "It would seem you know me better than I know myself."

"Oh, Jordan. Don't be mad at me," Monica pleaded. "I'm only trying to help. You're such a beautiful person. You have so much to offer, so much life to live, I just can't stand to see you throw it all away." She hesitated for a moment. "You realize that if you do, you're only finishing what Philip started."

Jordan jerked as though she'd been slapped. "What is that supposed to mean?"

"Just what I said. Philip punished you for his own inadequacies. He was selfish, cruel and sadistic, and he made your life hell on earth because of it. Now, you're punishing yourself for allowing it. But don't you see, Jordan? You never had any control over it. It was never your fault."

Jordan made a gesture of denial, but Monica continued determinedly, "I've been there, Jordan. I know what I'm talking about. I'll admit my marriage might not have been quite as . . . traumatic as yours. Rick slapped me around a few times, but he never put me in the hospital, and I still have my baby." Her eyes softened as she watched Angie playing at the table. "It was three years I don't ever want to live again, but that doesn't mean I've given up on living. I may even decide to get married again one day." She laughed halfheartedly. "I can promise you I'll be a lot more careful in my selection, but the point is I'm willing to try again. And that's the point I'm trying to make to you, Jordan. You've been using your memories as a shield, a shield that keeps the rest of the world at arm's length. Don't you think you've punished yourself long enough?"

Jordan was grateful for the kitchen stool behind her as she slid onto its cushioned top. "Do you think that's what I've been doing?" Her voice was low, her throat raw with suppressed emotion.

Monica nodded. "Yes. I didn't want to say anything; I was afraid I'd hurt your feelings. But after you told me about Lance Rutledge, I decided it was time I spoke up. As I told you before, guys like him come along only once in a

lifetime." She picked up her daughter and walked to the
back door. "Come on, cherub, I think we'd better go. We've
done enough damage for one morning."

Far more shaken than she cared to admit, Jordan stayed
where she was long after Monica and Angie left. Time had
no meaning as she sat there, letting Monica's words play,
then replay, in her mind. She was faced with a new image of
herself, and the image wasn't pretty.

Monica had painted the portrait of a coward—a coward
who hid behind her past. And it was true. All of it. She was a
coward, hiding from the world when it got too close. She
was afraid of people, afraid of their judgments, their con-
demnations, their curiosity. She'd been exposed to that
before, the whispers and the speculation, and had vowed
that her life would never be open to public inspection again.
Not to family, not to friends—a vision of Lance's smiling face
came to her—not to anyone.

But maybe it was time to make some changes. Though
she knew she wasn't up to anything major, like an instant
love affair or an involved relationship, perhaps her life could
do with a few alterations.

There was one relationship she definitely wanted to
preserve. Before she could change her mind, she walked to
the wall phone and punched out a familiar number. Grip-
ping the receiver tightly, she listened to the buzzing at the
other end of the line.

"Monica," she said quickly when the phone was answered. "I wanted to say thank you . . . for being a friend
. . . a good friend. I didn't want you to think I was angry. I
appreciate what you were trying to do. And, Monica, one
more thing. I'll try to keep an open mind about Lance
Rutledge."

The next morning, Jordan was awakened by the sound of
distant pounding. She stirred groggily, opened her eyes a slit
and peered at her bedside clock. It was too early to get up,
she decided, and burrowed deeper in the covers.

The pounding continued.

It had to be the front door. Muttering under her breath, she slid her feet to the floor and reached for the robe at the end of the bed. She threw it on, belting the sash as she went up the stairs. She'd been awake until the early hours of the morning, wrestling with her thoughts and memories, and almost felt sorry for whoever was at her door at this, to borrow Monica's phrase, ungodly hour. They were about to receive a greeting they'd never forget.

The heavy rapping sounded again.

"All right, all right. I'm coming," she yelled. Pushing back her tousled hair, she yanked open the front door. "Didn't you see the doorbell? All you had to do—" She broke off, the sight before her robbing her of speech.

Leaning casually against her porch rail, booted feet crossed at the ankles, arms folded over his chest, looking as tan and fit as ever, was Lance Rutledge.

"Good morning, Jordan. Did I wake you?"

His voice was just as she remembered it, soft, warm and a little husky. She was having trouble finding hers.

"Lance, what are you doing here?"

He straightened, and her eyes followed every movement. He was just as tall as she remembered, his body lean, rangy and muscled. Lord, Jordan, did you expect him to shrink or develop a pot belly?

"Didn't you get my note? I said I'd be here on the second." His brow creased in perplexity, and she anxiously studied his face. It was just as handsome as she remembered, with its warm brown eyes, straight nose, full, sensual lips. Her memory of his lips was especially vivid.

"Yes, I got your note, but I wasn't expecting you until late this afternoon. Didn't you take the shuttle from Santa Fe?"

He shook his head, and gold-tipped curls fell across his forehead. "No, I flew myself. That's why I'm here so early."

He shrugged dismissively, and that, too, was just as she remembered, the easy acceptance, the confidence and the unpretentiousness.

"You flew? You have a license?"

He smiled, and it was the smile that she remembered. It softened the lean planes of his face, lit his eyes and crinkled their corners. And its effect on her was still the same . . . devastating.

"Yes, they won't let you fly without one." He paused and glanced around him. "You've got a great place here. It's even more impressive than I expected it to be." He looked pointedly over her shoulder. "Do you think I might come in?"

She jumped backwards as though she'd been shot, and warm color tinted her cheeks.

"I'm sorry. Please come in." She opened the door wider. "I didn't mean to keep you standing out on the porch."

"Porch," he said with a smile as he picked up his luggage and walked past her into the entryway. "That's a word I haven't heard in a long time. Reminds me of Texas."

"Porch? Don't the houses in California have porches?"

"No. You hear about decks or patios or terraces, or maybe someone's balcony, but nothing as common as a porch." He set his cases on the floor and turned to face her. "It's good to see you again, Jordan."

His gaze traveled leisurely down her body and she shifted self-consciously from one bare foot to the other, acutely aware of her state of undress. She tugged at the front of her robe with one hand while she tried to smooth her hair with the other.

"I must look a fright," she apologized nervously. "I wasn't expecting anyone so early. I was still in bed and when I heard the pounding on the door, I didn't take time—"

"You look fine to me," he interrupted. "As beautiful as ever." He reached out to calm her, and his touch was as gentle as she remembered.

She stepped away from him and drew a shaky breath. "I think I'd better make some coffee."

He followed her down the staircase to the den and she

pointed to a sofa. "Make yourself comfortable. I'll only be a minute."

Jordan turned and headed down another staircase. The house was built on the side of a mountain and therefore sprawled onto several levels, the kitchen being on the lowest. Most women would think its placement appropriate, but Jordan often wished it were more centrally located. She loved to cook, and usually found it relaxing. This morning, though, she felt all thumbs as she measured coffee and poured water into the coffeemaker.

The chore completed, she rested her head against the cabinet. Why did he affect her this way? She felt as though she were sixteen again and going to her first party. What was it about the man that upset her equilibrium like this? Wasn't he only flesh and blood, bone and muscle?

"Jordan, are you all right?"

She jumped. He was so close that his breath fanned her hair. She hadn't even heard him enter.

"Yes, I'm fine. I guess I'm still a little sleepy."

"I shouldn't have wakened you so early, but I was anxious to see you again."

"That's okay. I'm usually up by now." She began taking cups and saucers from the cabinet. "I think the coffee's ready. How do you like yours?"

"Black is fine." He walked to the table and took a seat. "Have you been getting a lot of writing done?"

She handed him his cup. "Quite a bit. You?"

"Not as much as I should have. I'm easily distracted these days."

"Oh." How was she supposed to answer that? Safer to change the subject. "Have you eaten? I could fix breakfast."

"I'd like that. The service was terrible on the Cessna."

Grateful for something to do, she walked to the refrigerator. She'd thought the strain of being with him was bad enough while she was in California. Having him here, in her home, was infinitely worse.

She took out eggs, butter and bacon and set them on the counter. Then she searched her mind for a neutral subject.

"How long have you been a pilot?"

"Legally or illegally?"

"Legally, I suppose."

"I got my license when I was sixteen, but I'd been flying a long time before that. My father had a small plane. To me, learning to fly it wasn't much different than learning to drive the family car."

"Your family must be wealthy," she said, then could have bitten out her tongue. "To own their own plane, I mean."

"Comfortable, not wealthy," he corrected. "And it wasn't that much of a plane. Just a little single-engine job. He used it to oversee the cattle."

"Just to oversee the cattle," she mocked, then smiled at his expression. "Sounds a little . . . haughty."

His laugh was rueful. "I guess it did, didn't it. That's not the way I meant it."

"I know." She laid strips of bacon across the heated skillet. "That's one of the first things I noticed about you."

She had his complete attention. "And that was?"

"Your lack of conceit. That's very unusual in someone of your reputation."

"Let's don't go into reputations right now." His voice was dry as he rose and walked to the coffeemaker. "What else did you notice about me?"

"Fishing?" she asked.

He poured his coffee, then moved to stand behind her, peering over her shoulder as she turned the bacon. "Would it get me anywhere if I was?"

"Probably not," she said lightly, but heard the tension in her voice. It was happening again. He stood so close that she could feel his heat emanating through his clothes. His coffee-scented breath warmed her cheek and teased her senses. His hands settled on her shoulders as though to turn her toward him, and she was ready. She'd been expecting him to touch her since he'd arrived, and she found herself wanting it, looking forward to it, perhaps—if she were honest—even needing it.

He was going to kiss her. She was sure of it. His hands on her shoulders turned her toward him, but only slightly. His lips hovered over hers for a moment, then parted, his breath mingling headily with hers.

"Jordan," he said, and his voice was rough. "Jordan, I think the bacon's burning."

"Oh, my God!" She yanked away from him and jerked the skillet from the burner. The smell of scorched meat burned her nose, its smoke burned her eyes. She quickly switched on the overhead vent. She thought she heard a soft chuckle as Lance walked back to the table, but in her confusion she couldn't be certain. He was right; the bacon was burning. Unfortunately, that wasn't all. Her face was flaming. She'd made a complete fool of herself, again.

"Can I do anything to help?"

She bent to pull a clean skillet from under the counter, careful to keep her back to the rest of the room. It was easier to deal with her embarrassment if she didn't have to face him. "No," she answered stiffly. "I think I can handle it."

But that was the problem, could she handle it? She didn't understand herself anymore. What was happening to her? Where was her common sense? She was beginning to think she no longer knew the woman that lived inside her body. She'd all but asked Lance to kiss her. The woman she used to know would never have done that.

She smiled wryly as she laid fresh bacon in the heated skillet. Monica was going to be very happy.

Though he was silent, she could feel Lance's gaze on her back as she continued cooking. When the bacon was ready, she took it out of the pan and put it on paper towels to drain. Then she put on a cheery smile and turned to face him.

"One catastrophe over and done with," she said brightly. "Now on to the next one. How many eggs do you want and how do you like them?"

"Two, and over easy." His voice was soft.

"Well, I'll see what I can do, but I'm not making any promises."

"Are you sure I can't do something to help?"

She cracked eggs and slid them gently into the skillet. "As a matter of fact, you can. How are you at fixing toast?"

He joined her at the counter. "That's probably the only thing I can fix. Point me to the toaster."

She watched as he slipped slices of bread into their slots and pushed the lever. "You did that very well," she told him.

"Yeah," he agreed. "And if this thing's set right, I may not even burn them."

She turned back to her skillet. "Is this your first time in Ruidoso?"

"No, I came here a few times with my parents when I was a kid. My dad was a sucker for the horse races."

"He'd enjoy this weekend, then. They run the American Futurity today. It's the biggest race of the year." She flipped the eggs over gently. "I had a hard time finding you a room because of it."

"A room?" His voice sounded different somehow.

"Don't worry," she assured him. "It's a nice place. I didn't put you up in a fleabag."

"That's reassuring."

Again, that note in his voice.

"Is something wrong, Lance? Had you made other arrangements?"

"No, not really." He carried the toast to the table. "It's just that I figured I would stay here with you."

She almost dropped the plate she was holding. "But Lance, you can't stay here."

"Why not?"

Every muscle in her body tensed. "Because"—her mind whirled with reasons—"you can't, that's why. How would it look?"

"To whom?" he returned reasonably.

She set his plate on the·table. "To everyone, of course. Especially my neighbors."

She couldn't let him stay with her. Surely he could see that.

"I quit worrying about what people thought of me years ago." He pulled a chair away from the table and sat down. "Besides, I didn't see any neighbors when I drove up."

"Well, I have neighbors. I've rented the apartment over my garage to a woman with a small child. How would it look to her if I let you stay?"

She knew how it would look. Monica would love it!

He looked up at her. "How small a child?"

He wanted specifics? "Small," she repeated.

He raised a questioning brow at her answer.

"Fifteen months," she admitted. "But she notices everything around her. Besides, Monica would know. Even if you're not worried about your reputation, think about mine."

"Jordan, be reasonable. We're both adults and we're both writers. I came here to work. People will understand that."

"Yes, but I'm a single woman. People are brutal when it comes to our reputations."

He watched her walk to the window. "True, but if we were bent on fooling around, we could do it just as easily in the daytime as at night. People are going to talk no matter what you do. Don't you know that by now?"

"Yes, I know that, but I still think it would be better if you weren't actually staying here." She turned to face him. "Besides, the motel is just a few miles down the road, right on the highway. It can't take over five minutes' travel time to get there."

"I didn't come here to travel," he protested. He knew he was pushing too hard, but couldn't help himself. "I'm a writer. I don't work at set hours, and I'm certainly not used to shuttling back and forth from a roadside motel. What am I supposed to do if I get an inspiration at two o'clock in the morning?"

That's exactly what I'm afraid of, she thought wryly. "All right, all right. You can stay," she told him, giving in. Hadn't she known all along she would? "But there have to be rules and you have to abide by them."

His shrug was casual for someone who felt like jumping up and clicking his heels together. "Your house, your rules," he conceded.

She watched him closely, unable to tell if he was being honest or mocking. She narrowed her eyes at him. "First of all, the only reason I'm agreeing to this . . . this arrangement is for the sake of the script."

"Business only," he agreed solemnly. "I can understand that."

"I don't mean monkey business."

"Of course not. Strictly business."

Again, she shot him a narrowed glance. "Secondly, is the division of labor. As you've no doubt noticed, I don't have a Mrs. Talmadge to take care of me. I do my own cooking, cleaning and laundry. Since this is strictly a business arrangement, I will expect you to carry your share of the household burden."

"My fair share," he said, nodding his head. "I wouldn't have it any other way."

"You're certainly being agreeable." She couldn't resist the comment.

His voice was relaxed. "As I said before, your house, your rules. Do I have a choice?"

His passivity aroused her suspicions, even as he managed to appear innocent. She didn't picture him as a man who lived easily with rules and regulations. She walked to the table and took a seat, gazing with distaste at her now cold breakfast. She glanced at Lance and found him watching her.

It was then that she was hit by the enormity of her decision. She had invited a man to share her house, her table, and for at least a short period of time, her life. The realization left her weak, shaken and more than a little astounded.

Monica was going to have a field day with this.

She'd promised to keep an open mind about Lance, but this . . .

She shook her head and, with a sigh of resignation, gave herself up to living, albeit temporarily and platonically, with a man for the first time in eight years.

7

So much could change in just a week. After seven days of living with Lance Rutledge, Jordan was convinced that she'd never be the same again. And the surprise of it all was that she was enjoying herself, actually having fun. To most people that wouldn't seem unusual, but to someone whose life had been singularly lacking in joy, it was a positive wonder. Whether it was because of the novelty of the situation, or because she was as susceptible to Lance's charms as any other female, she didn't know. The only thing clear to her was that she felt more uniquely alive than she had in ages.

Lance was good company. They laughed, they talked, they even argued. He fascinated her, tantalized her, even while he provoked her. He made the difficult seem easy, and the common seem exciting. And he was so darned unpredictable that she was finding there was no way to second-guess him. The easiest thing to do, she'd decided, was just go along for the ride.

She watched him now as he slept, peacefully sprawled

across her sofa. A morning in town, shopping and running errands, had worn him out, he had claimed as he settled down to watch Saturday afternoon baseball. He'd lasted at least five minutes before falling asleep.

It felt strange, watching him when he was most vulnerable, incapable of defending himself and unable to watch her in return, but it was oddly satisfying too. She thought he always looked younger than the thirty-four years she knew him to be, but in repose, he looked younger still, more relaxed, as though at peace with the world.

She was amazed that he was still roaming around single and unattached. Monica had told her that his name had been linked with the names of some of the most glamorous women in Hollywood. It was a wonder one of them hadn't already snapped him up. . . . No, that was wrong. Lance had too much strength of character to be snapped up by anyone. The choice would always be his.

That made his being there in her home all the more puzzling. He didn't need her help to write the script. After seeing how he worked this past week, she was more certain of that than ever. That meant his reason for being there had to be personal, but she found no comfort in the knowledge. She knew she was being selfish, but she wasn't ready for anything stronger or deeper than friendship.

On the whole, though, Lance made accepting their situation easier for her. There were even times when she thought she might have misjudged him. He'd been a perfect houseguest—thoughtful, considerate and well behaved. And though there had been times she'd had the feeling that he wanted to, he had not tried one overt move in her direction. He'd been charming, polite and entertaining, without a single hint of pretense or deception. She smiled as she remembered one of their first conversations and wondered if it had any influence on his behavior.

After breakfast that first morning, Lance had requested a tour of the house and grounds. Jordan had been happy to oblige. She was proud of her home and, since she didn't have many visitors, didn't get many opportunities to show it off.

"This place is fantastic," he had told her after they'd toured the house and were standing in the backyard looking out over her valley. "How many acres do you have?"

"Forty," she had answered. "Do you see that row of pines just beyond the creek bed?" He nodded. "That's my property line."

"I'm impressed. We have a woman of means here."

"Forty acres hardly makes a woman of means, but I'm proud of it." Her gaze swept the familiar landscape. "It's the first place I've ever owned."

"It doesn't worry you, living alone, so far out of town?"

She tilted her head, a quizzical line appearing between her brows. "No. Why should it?"

He frowned. "I'd think that would be obvious; you're a single woman, several miles from town, virtually unprotected."

"Oh, Lance," she chided. "You don't have to worry about me. This place is well protected. I have a very sophisticated alarm system, which, by the way, I'd better show you how to operate since you're going to be staying here. It's tied in to the police station and I'd hate to have to come bail you out sometime."

"An alarm system takes care of the house. What about you personally?"

"I can take care of myself."

His look held disbelief. "Sure you can. What happens if the alarm fails? What happens in the ten to twenty minutes it takes the police to arrive? What happens if you're attacked outside the house? What then, Jordan? Can you still take care of yourself?"

"As a matter of fact, yes. It just so happens I'm an excellent marksman."

"I didn't see any guns in the house."

She threw him a wry look. "You weren't supposed to."

He digested that for a moment. "That's good—that you

know how to use a gun, I mean. But you realize, of course, that guns are not the answer to every security problem."

"I know that's true," she agreed. "And I always try to exercise caution whether I'm at home or away. I've tried to utilize every safeguard and precaution available to me. I had the alarm system installed after I bought the house, special locks put on all the doors and windows and security lights hung outside the house. I even joined Neighborhood Watch."

"Very commendable, but there are still times—"

She laid her hand on his arm. "Lance, I'm not unaware of the dangers to a woman living alone, and I appreciate your concern, but I've lived alone for several years now. I think I can take care of myself."

He walked to the back door and slid open the screen, but hesitated before entering. "A marksman, huh? I've never known a female sharpshooter before. Should I call you Annie Oakley now?"

She remembered his love of the early western movies and couldn't restrain the smile that tugged at her lips. "Hardly. As you can see, I don't carry a six-gun strapped to my hip."

His eyes moved to that part of her anatomy. "No," he said, regarding her with sober interest, "but something tells me you're still lethal."

Another surprise, Jordan found, was Lance's domesticity. She had already resigned herself to the extra household burden a guest-in-residence represented. She knew from experience that men and housework were not compatible. Philip had never lifted one finger in the house during their entire four years of their marriage, and her father hadn't been much better when she was at home. So it came as no small surprise that Lance was not only willing to help, but was quite proficient in most areas. His room and bath were always spotless, he was a whiz at washing dishes and running the vacuum and, much to Jordan's consternation, he even tried his hand at laundry. She had found him in the laundry room one day sorting clothes, and had almost fainted with embarrassment when she recognized her underwear in a frothy pile in the corner.

"Lance, I know we decided on a fair division of labor," she had said when she finally recovered her voice, "but it's not necessary for you to do the laundry. I'll handle that."

"Oh, it's no problem," he had returned. "I'm pretty good at this. Ina showed me how so that I can do mine when she's not around. I know all about sorting and treating stains and setting the water temperature. One thing, though." And his gaze indicated the pile of feminine apparel in the corner. "I will leave those for you. I don't have any experience with ladies lingerie—at least not in washing them."

She had fled then, but the sound of his delighted chuckle had followed her down the hallway.

The only fault she could find with Lance's household skills was his pitiful performance in the kitchen. Anything past washing dishes was beyond him. She'd often heard of people who couldn't boil water, and Lance was a prime example.

They had agreed the first day to take turns with the preparation of meals, but by the end of the week, Jordan was ready to throw in the towel. For lunch the first day, she'd prepared tuna crescents. That night, she had served teriyaki chicken with rice pilaf. For lunch the second day, Lance had served bologna sandwiches and taken her out to dinner. The third day, Jordan had chopped up a large chef salad for lunch and served it with her special homemade dressing. The dinner menu that night had included beef stroganoff served over buttered noodles, with strawberry cheesecake for dessert. The fourth day, which was Lance's day, started off with corn flakes for breakfast, frozen pot pies for lunch and dinner at an Italian restaurant.

It was easy to see a pattern developing, and when Jordan had insisted she was too tired to go out for dinner on the sixth night, he'd brought it home instead. Fish and chips served in paper cartons. When she'd asked about dessert, his eyes had lit triumphantly. Going back to the kitchen, he had returned with a small sack and pulled out a six-pack of Snickers.

"You didn't think I'd remember dessert, did you?" he questioned, tossing her a candy bar.

She looked at the paper-wrapped package in her hand and had the strongest desire to burst out laughing. Contrarily, she also felt a strange urge to cry. His gesture had been sweet, thoughtful and oddly touching. As she tore away the wrapper it occurred to her that this was the first time a man, any man, had brought her candy.

Lance might not have been much of a cook, but he was an excellent scriptwriter. Her only complaint was that his way of working was unorthodox. She was used to set hours, and he preferred to "flow," as he called it, working when the mood and inspiration moved him. She soon learned that "flowing" could mean working two or three hours one day and twelve hours the next.

What she couldn't complain about, though, was the result of his "flowing." Lance was quick and creative, more so than she'd even imagined, and the script was beginning to take shape much the way she'd originally envisioned it. And though it was a challenge, requiring a different style and a different technique, she was finding that she enjoyed working on the teleplay and seeing something she'd written develop from a new angle.

The script was going to be good. She could feel it in her bones. Lance had a genius for slicing straight through to the heart of the matter in as few words as possible. He could reduce scenes that had originally filled pages to a paragraph, a sentence or a few words of dialogue.

Her instincts about him as a writer had been correct. She was convinced, now more than ever, that she'd made the right decision in insisting on Lance as screenwriter.

Her musings were interrupted as Lance stirred, and she watched first one lid lazily lift, then another. As his gaze slowly focused, the smile that had teased his lips in sleep slowly deepened. He yawned and stretched contentedly.

"Guess I drifted off for a while."

"Looks that way," she agreed.

He peered at the television. "Game's already over?"

"You slept right through it."

"Who won? The Dodgers?" His voice was hopeful.

She shook her head. "Houston. Three to two."

He groaned.

"Hey, I thought you were a Texan," she admonished.

"I am, and I'd root for Houston if they weren't playing the Dodgers."

"Ah, such loyalty," she teased him. "It's overwhelming."

"I'll tell you what's overwhelming," he said, swinging his feet to the floor and heading to the kitchen. "My appetite. Must be all this mountain air. I've eaten like a horse since I've been here."

She smiled at his back as she followed. "I noticed that, too."

"Don't be sarcastic," he warned, his head inside the pantry. "It doesn't become a lady." He closed the cabinet door and walked to the refrigerator. "What's on the menu tonight? If my memory serves me right, it's your night to cook." He pulled out an overripe banana and began to peel it.

She shuddered as he took a bite of the spotted fruit. "Yuk, Lance. Wasn't there a fresher banana in there?"

He nodded as he swallowed. "Yeah, but this is just how I like 'em."

She shook her head and walked to the refrigerator. "It's just as well you're hungry now. I was planning on an early dinner. I have plans for later."

His brows arched and were almost lost in the mop of curls that covered his forehead. "What kind of plans?"

She took out a package of ground beef and laid it on the counter. "Baby-sitting, actually. Monica called while you were asleep, and she has a date with Glenn tonight." She pulled out a jar of pickles and a head of lettuce. "She asked if I could watch Angie."

"That's great," he said without hesitation.

His answer surprised her; she couldn't tell whether he was being honest or mocking. "Look, you don't have to stay around here tonight if you don't want to. You could take my car and go into town. It is Saturday night, after all."

"What's this? Are you trying to get rid of me? I must be losing my touch if you're tired of me already."

"Don't be silly. It isn't anything like that. It's only that Angie is just over a year old and she still gets messy sometimes and a little cranky if things don't go her way."

"Sounds like a normal kid to me. So what's the problem? Do you think I don't like children?"

She turned her attention back to the contents of her refrigerator. "I don't know, do I? You've only met Angie once, and that was briefly. You might have an aversion to spending Saturday night at home with a fifteen-month-old."

Taking her arm, he pulled her to him, and closed the refrigerator door behind her. "I don't care where or how I spend Saturday night as long as I'm with you, even if we have to take care of a dozen kids. For your information, I happen to like children. I plan on having a house full of my own someday."

She tried to picture him surrounded by a brood of rowdy children, each with gold-tipped curls and penetrating brown eyes, and was surprised when the picture easily came into focus.

"You might find that Angie is a little spoiled."

"That's okay. I think I can handle one little girl."

"As long as you know what you're letting yourself in for."

His hands cupped her face. "I think I've always known what I was in for."

He was doing it again! His dark gaze seemed to pierce her very soul. She took an instinctive step backwards, but he followed. She could feel the cold metal of the refrigerator against her back.

"Lance, you don't . . . I didn't . . . you promised . . ."

"I promised not to do anything you didn't want me to." He pulled back a fraction. "Don't you want me to kiss you?"

The decision was hers. The answer should have been easy, but it wasn't. Her heart wouldn't cooperate with her mind. She felt confused, pulled in two directions, yet inexplicably drawn to this man.

Her heart was in her throat as she opened her mouth to speak. No sound emerged. His gaze was still intent on hers.

"That's what I thought," he said and lowered his head to hers.

His lips met hers softly, yet firmly, and Jordan felt a delicious shiver run the length of her spine as his tongue pushed gently past her lips to probe and explore the inner recesses of her mouth. He caught her bottom lip between his teeth, and an avalanche of sensation cascaded through her. She clutched at his shoulders, needing his support, and felt the hard strength of his body as his arms lowered to hold her close.

Desire throbbed between them instantly. He deepened the kiss, demanding her response, abolishing her reluctance. He gave her no time to think or to reason, only to react. She moaned low in her throat as his hands moved to rest at the sides of her breasts. His palms rotated softly against the sensitive skin, and she felt herself swell and expand at his touch. She wanted him to touch her. Needed him to touch her.

The kiss seemed to last forever. His mouth pressed down on hers, hungry, demanding and totally intoxicating. Through the silken texture of her blouse, she could feel his fingers massaging, stroking, exploring. His lips left hers to trail soft, moist kisses over her face and neck, and she trembled, knowing she should stop him, but too weak to make the effort.

When had anything ever felt this good?

But it was madness. Somehow she had to put a stop to this . . . this sweet torture.

"Lance."

He lifted his head as she said his name, but only for a moment. His lips began a sensual journey across her forehead, down to her temple, then on to her cheek.

"Don't," she whispered unsteadily.

"Why not?" he murmured against her skin.

She could hardly breathe, much less answer. "You're not supposed to be doing this. You promised."

"Did I? I don't remember."

"Lance, we had an agreement. No monkey business!"

He raised his head at that. "Monkey business? That's the first time I've ever kissed anyone and been accused of that!"

She pulled away from him and walked unsteadily to the window. "I'm sorry if that sounded prudish. I can't help it; that's just the way I am."

"Don't worry about it," he said, and his voice was calm. "A momentary lapse on my part. I'm back to gentlemanly behavior. What's for dinner, by the way?"

She hated that he could sound so unperturbed when her knees were still shaking. "Nothing gourmet," she answered wrathfully. "We're having hamburgers."

"Great, I love hamburgers. Need any help?"

"No, I think I can manage." She needed time. Time for thinking, sorting, stabilizing. "Why don't you go watch television or something? I'll let you know when it's ready."

Brown eyes gleamed at her. As usual, he'd seen through her ploy. "Okay. Just call if you change your mind."

She watched him saunter from the room before sagging against the window frame. She lifted a hand to smooth back her hair and realized it was shaking. He'd done it again. He'd gone through her defenses as if they weren't even there. How could she convince him that she didn't want to get involved with him or anyone else when she melted like butter every time he touched her?

Obviously, the real problem was with herself. And as with any other problem, she reasoned, she'd simply have to find a way to work through it.

She walked to the sink and began sorting through the ingredients for their dinner. The flaw in her reasoning, she admitted as she shaped ground beef into patties and set them aside, was that she'd been giving herself the same advice for over a month and it hadn't worked yet.

They were just finishing dinner when Monica breezed in the back door, Angie under one arm, a canvas tote under the other. Lance immediately rose from the table to help. Jordan was surprised when he reached for the squirming child instead of the bag.

"Oh, Jordan, you're a dear," the redhead began as Jordan took the tote from her. "Becky Dodson was supposed to baby-sit tonight, but she called this afternoon and canceled. I didn't know who else to call on such short notice."

"That's fine, Monica. No problem," she answered distractedly. Her eyes were on Lance and the child. "We're glad to help out. Can I fix you something to drink?"

"Oh, no, thanks. I'm running late."

Anyone who knew Monica knew she was always running late, and Jordan shook her head. "Slow down; Glenn will wait." She filled a glass with iced tea and handed it to her friend. "Where are you two going tonight?"

Monica opened her mouth to answer, then gaped comically as she looked from Jordan to Lance. "Oh, my gosh! I bet you two had plans! I didn't even think to ask you. I guess I'm just not used to you ever going out . . . oh, Jordan, you should have said something. I'm so sorry. I'll take her back with me—"

Embarrassed by Monica's ramblings, Jordan hastened to assure her. "No, it's all right. We hadn't planned on anything."

"Are you sure? I'm so scatterbrained sometimes. I should have thought about this being Mr. Rutledge's first weekend here."

"Hey, none of that Mr. Rutledge stuff," Lance interrupted. "It's just Lance, and Jordan's right. We hadn't planned on going out tonight. It's been a long week. I think we both would like a quiet evening at home."

Jordan's pulse leaped at the way he said "at home," but warned herself to take it easy. She concentrated on being casual. "Besides, Monica, after L.A., I don't think Ruidoso's night life would hold much appeal for him."

Monica laughed. "You're probably right, but you won't get much of a quiet evening with this one around." She reached over Lance's shoulder to chuck her daughter under the chin. Her breasts brushed against Lance's arm and Jordan held her breath, waiting for his reaction. There was none.

If he noticed the gesture at all, he gave no sign. He continued playing with the baby and Jordan released her breath on a shaky sigh. She had wondered what Lance's response to the lovely redhead would be and didn't know whether to be relieved or irritated that there wasn't any. This was their second meeting, and while Monica had gazed at him with an awed expression at their first meeting, nothing monumental had transpired. Lance had been friendly and polite, but almost dismissive. His attitude seemed no different now.

"Go ahead, Monica," Jordan told her. "Have a good time. We'll be fine. I'll put Angie to bed over here and you can pick her up in the morning."

"Jordan, you're a doll! What would I do without you?" Monica leaned over to kiss her daughter good-bye and brushed a kiss across Jordan's cheek as well before heading for the back door. "I'll see you in the morning."

Except for Angie's gurglings as she played in Lance's lap, the kitchen was silent after Monica's departure. Jordan held her breath waiting for Lance to comment on Monica's reference to her dating habits, or the lack thereof, certain that he would take it as further proof that she was indeed Rachel.

Nervously, she began stacking dishes from the table. When Lance stood, she hastily carried the stack to the sink, but when she turned back toward the table, he was standing right behind her.

Their gazes met for a long moment before he thrust the child at her. "Here. I think Angie could do with a dry diaper. You take care of her and I'll handle KP duty."

Jordan accepted the child gratefully and fled to the room she had affectionately dubbed as Angie's. By the time she had changed the baby's diaper and buttoned her into pajamas, Angie was yawning sleepily. She was out for the count as soon as Jordan laid her on her tummy in the secondhand baby bed she'd bought for her.

Jordan tiptoed from the room and gently pulled the door closed behind her, then squealed when she backed into a warm, solid form standing behind her. Lance's hands curved firmly around her shoulders, steadying her.

"Sshh, it's just me," he whispered close to her ear. "Come on into the den. I made us a drink."

She allowed him to lead her back down the staircase, but stopped dead in her tracks when she saw that the only light in the room came from the fireplace.

"A fire? In September?"

Lance's grin was unrepentant. "It felt a little chilly to me; besides, it's a great way to save on electricity." He tugged on her hand. "Come on. See what I made for us."

She eyed the darkened room and steaming mugs on the fireplace hearth with trepidation. Here it comes, she told herself dismally. The big seduction scene, complete with hot toddies and flickering firelight.

She licked lips that had suddenly gone dry. "Lance, I don't think this is a very good idea—"

He held out a mug to her. "Do you like marshmallows?"

"Marshmallows?" He should have been a baseball pitcher, she thought numbly. He certainly knew how to throw a curve.

"Yeah. What's hot chocolate without marshmallows?"

How could he keep doing it so consistently? Perhaps the question should be how could she keep doing it so consistently? How could she keep sticking her foot in her mouth every time she opened it around him?

She started to turn away from him, away from the knowing look and mocking smile, but he gently pulled her down to the carpet beside him.

"Come sit by me and drink your cocoa. You don't have to be so suspicious, you know. I keep telling you how trustworthy I am; maybe now you'll believe me." His gaze was gentle on her face. "I thought it might be nice just to sit here in front of the fire and talk."

"Yes. I always enjoy a fire." She took an experimental sip of her chocolate. "Mmmmmm . . . that's not bad. For such a lousy cook, you make great cocoa."

"It was instant."

"Figures," she said and they both laughed.

"You don't do that often enough," he said when they sobered.

She stretched her feet out toward the fire. "What?"

"Laugh."

She looked away self-consciously. "I laugh when there's something to laugh about."

"Maybe that's the problem then."

"Do I seem sad to you?"

He studied her for a long moment. "Not sad, exactly. Too serious maybe."

She stared into the flames. "I'm sorry if I seem boring to you. I did warn you, though."

His fingers under her chin turned her to face him. "Did I say you were boring?"

She turned away again. "No, but it's the same thing. You said I was too serious."

"I just like to see your smile." His fingers gently played down her neck to her shoulder, and down the silky length of her arm. "You're very beautiful in the firelight, do you know that?"

She shook her head. "I've never been beautiful in my life. The darkness has you fooled."

"Oh, no," he said, leaning closer until his breath fanned her cheek and its warmth made her tingle. "I've seen you at all times of the day and night. You're always beautiful. There are just some times I like better than others."

"You should see me at my worst," she said shakily.

"Like first thing in the morning?" She nodded. "I already have, remember?" His lips were only a breath from hers. "The morning I arrived you came to the door with your hair all mussed and not wearing any makeup. Your cheeks were pink and soft from sleep and it was easy for me to imagine waking up with you beside me looking like that."

"Don't . . ." she whispered.

"Don't what? Don't touch you? Don't kiss you? Don't love you?" He loomed above her and pushed her back against the carpet. "I'm sorry, Jordan. It's too late. I have to."

His mouth crushed down on hers then with an almost desperate hunger, a hunger she'd only had glimpses of before. His kiss was intoxicating, exhilarating and a little frightening, going beyond anything she had ever experienced or expected from a man. His tongue searched and probed, possessing her mouth as though he'd been starving for the taste of her. She moaned and clutched at his shoulders, but his mouth continued its sweet plunder, its eloquent exploration.

Heat coursed through her body as his lips slid to her throat, and his tongue played with the delicate hollow at the base of her throat. Her arms slid around his neck as restless hands roamed from her shoulders to her hips. An electric current, following the movement of his hand, pulsed through her body. It tingled down her spine as his fingers stroked under her shirt, quivered along her stomach as his hand traced a path to her navel, radiated down her thighs as his hand moved lower against her jeans.

His mouth traveled back to hers to sip and taste and nibble. She moaned against his lips but he continued the tender torture. Each touch sent a tremor of yearning through her until she was weak with her need for him.

"Lance," she began, but could not continue when he slipped his hands under her blouse. She felt his hands gliding up to cup her breasts and could only moan as pure sensation took over. His touch was so sure, so tender, how could she fight him?

He kneaded her gently. The rough scrape of his palms created a delicious friction against her sensitive skin. His head lowered, and his teeth worried open the buttons of her blouse. He buried his face in the fragrant valley between her breasts, letting his tongue tease and taste and tempt. When he raised his head, she moaned in protest.

"Open your eyes, Jordan." His voice was a rough whisper coming from just above her. "Open your eyes. I want you to look at me."

She forced her eyes to open. His face was so close that she could feel his breath warm her lips and his gaze touch her skin. His eyes were dark, intense.

"Tell me this is wrong, Jordan. Tell me you don't feel the same thing I do."

She shook her head and tried to bury her face in his shoulder, but his hands on her arms held her back. "Tell me, Jordan. I want to hear you say it. Tell me I shouldn't love you."

"You shouldn't," she whispered weakly against his chest. "You shouldn't."

"It's too late, damn you. It's too late." He crushed her lips under his, taking hers fiercely, savagely, desperately. One arm curved under her body, holding her against the hardness of his while the other pushed aside her blouse to seek and find her breast. She heard his groan of satisfaction as the nipple under his hand instantly began to tighten.

"You're mine, honey. Whether you want to admit it or not, you're mine."

Shock stilled her movements, her thoughts, her response.

Panic rippled through her. You're mine, he'd said. Possession. Ownership. God, what was she doing? Had she forgotten everything?

She began struggling against his hold, turning and twisting, trying to dislodge the arms that held her, but the weight of his body held her pinned against the floor.

"Let me go!" She heard the fear and panic in her voice. "Lance, please! Let me go!"

He levered his body away from hers, but retained his grip on her arms. "Jordan, don't do this. Listen to me. I'm not going to hurt you. Do you hear me?" He shook her slightly. "I'm not going to hurt you."

He rolled to his feet in one fluid motion, pulling her with him, and they stood facing each other. Her breath trembled from her. She was shaking from head to toe and her breasts still heaved with emotion. Seeing Lance's gaze shift to her breasts, she realized that her blouse was open and that the lacy material of her bra could not hide her from his visual examination.

She longed to cover herself and struggled to free her arms from his hold. But his grip was like a vice and she succeeded only in further parting the sides of her shirt.

Her head dropped to her chest. "Please let me go, Lance."

"You know I can't do that," he told her, then pulled her close against him, pressing her head into the hard curve of his shoulder. His lips brushed her forehead in a fleeting caress and his warm breath teased her sensitive skin as he murmured, "You don't have to hide yourself from me, or be ashamed for me to see you. You're beautiful, and all I want to do is love you."

She shook her head from side to side. "No. No, you can't."

"But I do. You know I do." He cupped her face with firm but gentle hands. "I love you, Jordan. And I think that deep inside, there's a part of you that loves me too."

She moaned and tried to shake her head but his hands held her steady.

"You can't change it by denying it, Jordan. You only postpone it. The outcome will be the same."

"You're wrong," she whispered, her voice rough with desperation. "You're wrong."

"Am I?" His hands framed her face, tilting it up as his lips descended to meet hers in a kiss so sweet, so seductive, that she found herself responding, answering, before she could think to protest. She almost whimpered when he drew away.

His mouth brushed across her cheek, and when he spoke she could feel his lips moving against her skin. "You may lie to yourself, but you can't lie to me. Your body won't let you. You want me just as badly as I want you. The only difference is that I'm honest enough to admit it and you aren't." She shivered as his tongue teased a damp, erratic path to the back of her ear. "See how it is? Even now you want me."

He stepped away from her then and she swayed without his support. "But it's your decision. I'll never force you. I'll even try to be patient. But I won't stop wanting you . . . or loving you."

8

Jordan's stomach churned ominously the next morning as she tried to force-feed herself a cup of coffee. Monica had arrived early to pick up Angie and was chatting nonstop about her date with Glenn. And though Jordan tried to respond normally, she realized that most of her answers were limited to grunts and nods.

"Hey, are you feeling all right?" Monica demanded when Jordan's lack of enthusiasm finally penetrated. "Come to think of it, you don't look too good."

Remembering the reflection in the bathroom mirror earlier, Jordan couldn't argue. The only color in her face had been the dark circles under her eyes that even makeup couldn't cover.

She managed a weak smile. "I didn't get much sleep last night."

Monica's brows rose speculatively. "Did Lance?"

"Good grief, Monica, I can't believe you'd ask such a question."

"You can't blame a person for wondering, and I for one certainly wouldn't blame you for taking advantage of a golden opportunity."

"I hate to disappoint you, but I'm afraid I've never been one to seize an opportunity. I've let several go by in my time."

"Well, there has to be a reason for your sitting here looking like you just fought World War III." She cast a suspicious glance at her daughter. "Did Angie keep you up? Was she fussy? I know she's been trying to cut another tooth, but I didn't think she'd keep you up all ni—"

"It wasn't Angie's fault, either," Jordan said, interrupting Monica's ramblings. "She was an angel, as usual, and slept all night." She sighed as she brushed her hair away from her face. "It's just me. I couldn't sleep. That's all there is to it."

"Well, whatever it is, I guess you'll work it out," Monica returned, unconvinced. "In the meantime, why don't you go back to bed and catch a nap? Surely you and Lance don't work on Sundays."

"No, we agreed to take off on weekends, but I don't think I could sleep if I lay down."

"Take my advice and try." Monica scooped up her daughter and walked to the back door. "Bloodshot eyes and dark circles are not attractive. Even on you."

Jordan remained seated at the table after the door closed behind Monica and Angie, but her thoughts were tangled, chaotic, and before long she found herself pacing. This isn't accomplishing anything, she admonished herself. It certainly doesn't solve the problem.

But she didn't know how to solve the problem, and her shoulders sagged in defeat as she forced herself to admit that.

In her heart, she knew that Lance Rutledge was a good man, a kind and honest man, a man with whom any woman could easily fall in love. He was the kind of man who made women think of wedding bells and long white dresses and living happily ever after. The kind of man she should have met when she was eighteen, while she was still young enough and idealistic enough to have enjoyed him.

But, as her mind took malicious pleasure in reminding her, she was no longer eighteen, and her days of youth and idealism were far behind her. Just because a man appeared to be kind and honest didn't mean that he was. Hadn't Philip presented the image of a perfect husband—kind, loving, considerate? And because no one knew of the nightmare she'd been living, hadn't everyone blamed her when she left him?

And hadn't she vowed that nothing, especially a man, would ever take her freedom away from her again? Hadn't she vowed to be independent, self-governing and self-reliant if she ever got away from Philip's hold? Then why, oh why, was it so hard to turn away from Lance Rutledge? Why had he come along to turn her life upside down?

She dropped her head into her hands. She forced back the tears that threatened, but couldn't force back the pain or the confusion that crowded her mind.

Suddenly, it was all too much. She had to get away. She needed time to think. After grabbing her jacket from its hanger by the door, she hurried outside and headed for the one place on earth that might offer her a small measure of peace.

Lance had noticed the small clearing earlier in the week on one of his dawn jogging excursions. It was nothing more than a ledge extending above the narrow stream Jordan insisted on calling a creek. Sheltered by a screen of pine and oak, the clearing was a natural haven, affording shade from the summer sun and protection from the north winds of winter.

And it was here that he found Jordan, head down, shoulders slumped, her arms wrapped around her knees. She looked small and defenseless, and he was hit by a fresh wave of guilt, knowing that he was responsible for that look.

Was he wrong to try to pull her from her shell? Did he have the right? But how long could she go on hiding from life? Hiding from herself? She had so much to give, so much love and warmth and passion, and he couldn't stop himself from wanting it all.

He dropped down beside her and saw her start of surprise. "Hey, is this a private meditation, or can anybody join?"

The smile she gave him was weak. "You're in luck," she answered. "Today's an open session."

He noted the dark smudges under her eyes and the pale shade of her skin against the midnight darkness of her hair, before purposely shifting his gaze to the serenity of the surroundings. "Looks like a good place for meditating. Quiet. Peaceful."

"I know. I guess that's why I come here so often. This place is sort of like your beach. It's one of the things that sold me on this place."

"I can understand that. I suppose everyone needs their own little corner, where they can go to be alone to think and work through their problems. I certainly use mine often enough."

She glanced at him sharply. "Really?"

"Why should that surprise you?"

"Oh, I don't know." She dug the toe of her shoe into the soft grass. "I guess you don't seem the type for quiet spots and meditation."

"What do I seem the type for? Night spots and swinging parties?" He shook his head. "You don't know me very well if you can think that, Jordan. I'm not a swinger at all."

He lay back against a bed of leaves and pine needles and threw one arm over his eyes, looking extremely comfortable and relaxed, and as though he had every intention of dozing off. Jordan watched in disbelief for a long moment before inquiring, "What are you doing?"

"What does it look like? I'm going to sleep. This is a perfect place for a nap." He removed his arm long enough to glance at her. "From the looks of you, you could use a little R and R, too. Why don't you stretch out and catch forty winks?"

"I . . . uh . . . here?" She looked around her.

"Sure, here. Why not?" His voice already sounded drowsy.

Why not? She tried hard but could not come up with a reason. She was tired, and the grass and leaves did look inviting. Why not, she thought again, and gingerly lay back on the natural carpet of soft grass.

Only a few minutes later, her eyelids began to grow heavier and heavier. The soft grass beneath her provided a comforting mattress, and soon she was dozing.

Her final memory was of rolling toward the warmth and comfort of Lance's body.

For Jordan, the next few days were harrowing. By Thursday, she was mentally and physically drained. Waking up in Lance's arms on Sunday afternoon had started the ball rolling, and it had been rolling continuously downhill ever since.

They had worked steadily on the script all week. And although Lance had not voiced his opinion aloud, Jordan soon realized that he hadn't changed his mind about her identity. He still believed she was Rachel, and everyday it became harder to convince him that she wasn't.

As they worked, memories—often dark, always painful—resurfaced. And though they were making good progress on the script, the strain of going back over it all had depleted her normal supply of patience and good humor, leaving her nervous and irritable.

Tension between them was thick, and frequent arguments erupted. She could feel one brewing now as they squared off over Lance's handling of a sensitive scene involving Rachel's apprehension over her pregnancy.

"You don't understand the intricacies of writing a screenplay or you'd understand why it has to be this way." He spoke with cool deliberation, but his anger was unmistakable.

"I know enough to know that you're butchering my book," she stormed, ready for battle. "You're deliberately making Rachel seem cold and uncaring about her unborn child when that's simply not the truth!"

"Damn it, Jordan, the audience can't stop and read three pages of introspection here! Facial expressions, body language, the actor's interpretation, those kinds of things have to convey the emotions and tell the audience what they need to know."

"I knew it was a mistake to sell the film rights to this book." Her words were sharp with fury. "I should have known it wouldn't work, even with you doing the writing."

Lance grabbed her shoulders. "Jordan, listen to me. No one is trying to butcher your book, least of all me. This is the way screenplays are written."

"Then I think they stink!"

"Don't you think you're getting too emotional, too involved with paper characters?"

Air hissed through her teeth. "Paper characters!" She jerked away from his hold. "They're more than paper characters!"

"Yes?" He was watching her closely.

Careful, Jordan, careful. You're getting near the edge, her mind screamed in warning. She had been living on nerves alone for the past several days and the stress was beginning to take its toll.

She backed away from him. "I . . . uh . . . I told you before that Rachel was a composite of hundreds of women and hundreds of cases. While she may be fictional, the people her character is based on are real. The same is true for the other characters in the book. They're all based on real people."

"I never doubted for a moment that they were," he countered.

Jordan struggled to keep her patience. "Lance, I want that

last scene rewritten. I think it's perfectly understandable that Rachel would be scared and apprehensive when she finds out she's pregnant. She has no future to look forward to. She's married to a man she fears and despises. Why would she want to bring a child into an environment like that?"

"That's exactly the way it's written. If you'd get your feelings off your cuff you'd be able to see it."

"Well, I don't see it and I want it rewritten. I won't approve this script until it is."

"Jordan, how can I rewrite it when that's the way it's already written?" He raked his hand through his hair in a gesture of frustration. "It's up to the director and the actors to interpret the emotions correctly."

"Do you think I'm going to leave it up to some actress's interpretation? Do you think I'd take that kind of chance?" She walked to the desk where they had been working and grabbed a handful of papers. "You're crazy if you think I'll let myself or my story be made a fool of on national television." She ripped the pages down the middle. The pieces fluttered to the floor. "I said it had to be rewritten."

Spinning on her heel, she headed for the door, but Lance was there ahead of her, his hand clamping down on hers on the handle. She thought of struggling, but his quiet voice stopped her.

"No, Jordan. You're not leaving. Do you think you can make such a grand gesture, then just walk out of here?" He shook his head. "I don't think so." He took her arm and pulled her back to the desk, giving her a helpful shove backwards into a chair. "If you want this scene rewritten, then you can damn well help rewrite it!"

Two hours later they were no closer to finishing the scene than they had been. They kept going back to the original version, and Jordan kept protesting until Lance finally threw down his pencil in disgust.

"There is no other way to write it, I tell you! This is exactly what we agreed upon that day in Durrell's office. I can't understand why you won't accept it now."

She was close to tears. "There has to be more feeling, more compassion. This isn't an ordinary story. Can't you see that?"

His voice gentled. "Yes, I see that. I also see that you're wearing yourself out over it."

A sigh, deep and heartfelt, escaped her lips. "I only wish you could understand why this scene must be handled with feeling and . . . sensitivity."

"The scene will work fine as it is; trust me on this. I wouldn't let anyone mishandle your story." She glanced at him quickly and he saw the question in her eyes. "My name's on the line, too. Remember?"

"It's more than just a matter of someone's name or reputation being on the line, Lance. We're talking about people's lives now. I agreed to allow this film to be made only because I hoped that someone else might benefit from Rachel's experiences."

"I understand that, Jordan, and I think your motives are admirable. But the fact remains that only if Rachel's story is told honestly and in depth can it help anyone. A glossed-over version will be useless."

Her anger resurged. "That's not fair! I wrote as complete and true a story as I possibly could. I didn't gloss over anything."

"In the book, no. That's why I don't understand your attempt to do it now." He raked impatient fingers through his hair. "The whole point of the book was to give people a hard look at the realities of wife abuse. And if we're to paint an accurate picture, we have to include the woman's true feelings, whether they're complimentary or not."

"I know that! And I agree. But gently! I don't want women to watch this and then feel guilty for having experienced the same feelings."

His expression suddenly tightened. "I think we're working at cross purposes here. I thought our objective was to raise public awareness on a subject that for too many years has been swept under the rug or hidden in the closet. I didn't realize our goal was to tranquilize victims."

Jordan leaped to her feet. "I should have known you wouldn't understand."

He watched her walk to the window. "Then explain it to me, Jordan. Tell me what I'm missing."

For long moments, she stood silently, continuing to stare out the window. He did not press her. When she did speak, her voice was low and controlled.

"Did you know that from one-third to one-half of all households in the United States have some type of abuse problem? And that battered wives outnumber all other abuse victims two to one? Unbelievable, isn't it?" She swung back to face him, and her face twisted. "Less than twenty percent of these cases are ever actually reported to authorities. That means the abusers go unpunished and the victims remain the silent sufferers.

"I have an obligation to those victims," she continued. "They live with fear and guilt, humiliation and degradation every day of their lives. I will not heap more on their heads. You're right. I do want to raise public awareness. I do want to bring the problem out of the closet and out from under the rug, but not at their expense."

Lance rose and walked toward her. "I understand your feelings for those women, Jordan, and I agree. But don't you see? Education is the best weapon against this type of violence. If the public gets a true picture of what's really going on, maybe they'll want to get involved and see that something's done about it. That's why this film needs to be as explicit as possible."

She recognized the logic of his words, but was still wary. He was still an outsider, after all. "What do you mean by explicit?"

"As realistic and in-depth as possible." Seeing the question in her eyes, he continued. "There are several very dramatic scenes in the book that should be transferred to the screen. The audience needs to experience everything Ra-

chel experiences, whether it's joy or sadness, fear or pain.
They need to see it, feel it, hear it, right along with her."

"You have particular scenes in mind?"

"Yes, as a matter of fact, I do. The scene we've just
finished is one of them."

"And the others?"

He hesitated for a moment, then spoke quickly. "All of
chapters nineteen and twenty."

His words drove the color from her face and the breath
from her body. She could only stand there, staring at him.
Afraid that her legs would not support her much longer, she
slowly made her way to the sofa and sagged weakly into its
welcoming depths.

She tried out her voice. "But that's . . . that's . . .
Rachel's final scene with her husband—the last beati—that's
when she loses her baby. Oh, Lance! You can't be thinking
of putting that on the screen!"

He dropped to his haunches in front of her and took her
hands in his. "Listen to me. That's the most emotional,
dramatic scene in the book. It's exactly what the audience
needs to see. The impact will be phenomenal!"

He looked at her steadily as he unrolled the scenario.
"Rachel resolves to get away. She sells what few pieces of
jewelry she has, packs her suitcase and hides it in the closet.
She plans to leave the following morning as soon as her
husband goes to work, thinking that will give her a full day's
headstart. But something goes wrong and he accidentally
finds the suitcase. He demands to know why it is there, and
Rachel, pushed to the breaking point, frustrated, disappointed and angry, loses all sense of caution. She blows up
and tells him she is leaving him, that she hates him and that
she never wants to see him again. He retaliates and hits
her . . . too hard and too often."

A taut silence followed his words. Tension vibrated
through the room, and when Lance continued, his voice was
husky with suppressed anger. "Somehow Rachel manages
to get away from him. She finds his car in the driveway, keys

in the ignition. She starts driving and even though she's badly hurt—even more seriously than she realizes—she's afraid to stop, afraid he'll catch up with her, so she keeps driving until the pain forces her to stop, alone, on the side of the highway. She wakes up the next day, in a strange room surrounded by strange faces, and realizes what has happened. She has lost her baby and, according to the doctor, almost her own life as well."

Jordan jumped to her feet, almost overbalancing Lance in the process, and walked to the desk. "All right! I get your point. I'm familiar with the story line, you know." She pushed trembling fingers through her hair. "It's just that I hadn't planned on the miscarriage scene being included."

He looked at her blankly for a moment. "Why not?"

"It's too personal."

"Personal?" His gaze glinted over her. "To whom?"

"To women in general, that's who," she returned sharply. "You just don't show something like that on national television!"

"Jordan, the situation will be handled very delicately. Nothing coarse or graphic. But this is an emotional story and it has to be handled as such. More important, it's an emotional story with a message. That's what made it special to begin with, and our job as writers is to make sure the message comes through loud and clear. We can't do that unless we make the emotions of the story work for us." Lance crossed the room to stand before her. "It will be handled sensitively. I promise you that. They won't film everything. Just enough to give it a feel of reality so that the audience will understand the extent of Rachel's anguish, suffer her loss with her. Otherwise, it's a secondhand experience."

Jordan's eyes widened. "You really are a heartless bastard, aren't you? You haven't heard a word I've said. I'm talking about people's lives and you're worried about audience participation!" She swallowed hard on the tears that threatened to choke her. "You're damn right it's an emotional book. Physical abuse is an emotional issue. But the book was written to expose the pain and suffering so many women have had to endure at the hands of men—not exploit it!"

"Don't use that word to me! You know that's not my intention!" His words sliced through the air.

She looked at him, standing there tall and proud and powerful, and knew her accusations were unfounded. Lance was an honest man, an honorable man, and she had charged him falsely.

She dropped her head, unable to meet his gaze. "I'm sorry," she whispered. "I shouldn't have said that."

"Forget it."

"No, I can't. I never talk to people like that and I'm really sorry I spoke so sharply to you. I didn't mean to call you . . . that name." She raised pleading eyes to his. "I know I'm too close to this story, and I know it affects my objectivity. It's just that I'm concerned. I want this film to help women, not add to their already heavy burden."

Lance took her shoulders and pulled her gently toward him. "I promised you from the beginning this would be a beautiful film; I haven't forgotten that promise. Trust me, Jordan. It's going to be a strong movie. I'll use every ounce of influence I have with Durrell to insure that it's produced just the way we've written it. One woman's triumph."

Countless seconds ticked by as she stood still and silent within his arms. Slowly she freed herself and walked to the door. "All right, Lance. It seems I've run out of options. We'll do it your way. I just hope and pray you know what you're doing." Quickly, she pulled open the study door and walked out.

Dinner that evening was a somber affair. It was Lance's day to cook, and being in no mood to look at a kitchen, he had elected to go out for dinner. The restaurant he had chosen specialized in flame-broiled steaks, and he watched now as Jordan pushed hers around her plate.

He wished she would eat. He'd watched pounds slide

from her slender frame that week, pounds she could ill afford to lose. Her weight loss, coupled with her lack of sleep, made her look small and fragile. She reminded him of the delicate little teacups that had sat in his grandmother's china cabinet when he was a child. They were hand-painted with intricate designs. He'd always wanted to hold one and examine it, but his grandmother had never allowed it, explaining that they could be crushed easily by just holding them in your hand. Now it seemed that Jordan had proven the truth of his grandmother's words.

He had recognized her fragility and vulnerability the first time he'd met her, but he'd also seen the strength and determination that was underneath. It was on that strength that he relied now.

They were having coffee before he decided it was time to broach the matter he'd been turning over in his mind all day. He tried to interest her in dessert first, but when she refused, he concluded that he might as well make his pitch.

He took a quick sip of coffee, then pushed it aside. "Jordan, I've been thinking. We both could use a break."

She gave him a cool look. "You're free to leave any time you want, Lance."

"No, that isn't what I mean. If I leave you here alone, you'll just work on that new book of yours, and I think you—we—both need some time off, away from books and scripts and writing altogether."

Considering the way she felt at the moment, she was inclined to agree. She busied herself adding cream to her coffee. "How long a break?"

"Just a few days," he answered. "Maybe a long weekend. That would probably give us enough time."

Her head snapped up at that. "Are you suggesting that we go away for a weekend . . . together?"

"Something like that." When she would have protested, he held up a hand. "Just hear me out before you go jumping to conclusions. My parents have a ranch near Brady, Texas.

They're always after me to come visit more often, and I thought since I was this close it would be a good opportunity to go see them. It would also be a good opportunity for us to take a break . . . together. We'd even be chaperoned. I think you'd like my folks, especially my mother. You remind me a lot of her. What do you say? It's only about four hours air time. If we left in the morning, we could be there by noon."

She silently considered his proposition. He was right about needing a break. She knew she would explode if she had to spend another day working on that script, not to mention working with Lance. It was quickly becoming an intolerable situation.

She looked at him across the rim of her coffee cup, silently wishing he weren't so attractive, so likable. Perhaps if he weren't it would be easier to turn him down. But as things stood now, she was neither ready to accept him nor reject him. Indeed, the thought of losing him turned her heart inside out.

Time, that was what she needed, and this weekend might be one means of obtaining it.

"All right, Lance," she heard herself saying. "A break it is. What time do you want to leave in the morning?"

When was the last time I did something just for the fun of it? Jordan wondered, watching the myriad of earth changes below her. She was enjoying the flight to Texas. Their plane was small but solid and the higher it soared, the lighter their moods became, forcing Jordan to realize that taking this weekend break was probably the best thing they could have done.

It wasn't until they landed that she felt her mood shift and some of her tension return. Lance saw and correctly interpreted her expression. Reaching across to help her unbuckle her seat belt, he squeezed her hand in reassurance.

"Come on, no frowns. They're just people; nothing for

you to get nervous about. They're going to love you." He turned away and snapped open his own belt, silently adding, *almost as much as I do.*

He opened the door and climbed to the ground, turning back to help Jordan do the same. A swirl of dust on the road below them indicated that they were soon to have company, and Lance leaned negligently against the wing strut, patiently waiting for their ride to the main house.

When the dusty Blazer bumped to a halt beside them, a tall, young man jumped out to greet them. With his warm brown eyes and devilish grin, he had to be Lance's brother. And if his looks weren't enough of a giveaway, his actions were. He immediately had Lance in a bone-breaking hug, thumping him on the back, while he laughed and talked at the same time.

"Damn, if you're not a sight for sore eyes," he said, holding Lance at arm's length for a quick inspection. "I didn't think you were ever coming back to Texas."

"It hasn't been that long," Lance protested.

"Long enough." The younger man pulled Lance back for one more hug and a couple more thumps before releasing him. "You're looking pretty good, big brother. A little soft, maybe, but I suspect that's due to all that easy living in California."

"Easy living?" Lance echoed. He jabbed at his brother playfully. "I can still take you anytime."

"Oh, yeah? I wouldn't bank on it if I were you," the younger man said, returning the poke.

Lance fended off the blow, then slipped an arm around his brother's shoulders. "Hey, hey. Settle down. I want you to meet someone special." He led the younger man over to Jordan, where she stood in quiet awe of the brothers' greeting. "Jordan Tyler Sinclair, meet my little brother, Clinton."

"Little?" He looked Lance up and down. "You've got to be kidding!"

"Well, younger, at least," Lance conceded. "My brother, at any rate."

She extended her hand to the younger man. "I'm glad to meet you, Clinton."

He took her hand, enfolding it in both of his. "Clint," he told her, staring into her face and pulling her slightly away from Lance. "Tell me, how did a lovely lady such as yourself get mixed up with a renegade playboy like my brother?"

She laughed but thought his description might be accurate. "It wasn't easy, I assure you." Then Lance was stepping between them, tugging their hands apart.

He retained his hold on Jordan's. "I'll thank you to keep your grubby hands off my woman, juvenile. If you must handle something, our cases are in the luggage compartment."

A few minutes later, Jordan found herself wedged between Lance and Clint in the front seat of the Blazer, bouncing over rocks and potholes as they wound their way down from the hilltop landing strip. Clint kept up a running monologue, but Jordan found it difficult to concentrate, and her attention kept wandering to the landscape surrounding her.

The countryside was beautiful. It was a vista of rolling hills and green meadows dotted with clumps of mesquite, pecan and oak. She could see cattle grazing in the distance, a mare and colt in a small pasture next to the road. It wasn't difficult to picture Lance in such surroundings. And since he habitually wore jeans and boots, she could easily imagine him astride some tall, proud stallion.

Lance's elbow nudged her back into the present. "Clint says mom and dad are waiting for us at the house, along with Abby and her crew. I hope you're ready for all of them."

"Abby?" she questioned.

"My sister. She's the middle child and the only girl."

She turned to Clint. "And you're the youngest?"

"Yeah, and the most spoiled," Lance answered for him.

Clint snorted. "I may be the most spoiled, but at least I stay and take it. You ran off to California."

There was a tense moment before Lance answered calmly, "I guess some of us are smarter than others."

The remainder of the drive was accomplished in near-silence, and Jordan was relieved to see the two-story brick house loom into view.

"Home, sweet home," Clint announced as they bumped to a stop in front of the house. He touched Jordan's arm before sliding from his seat. "Come on in. Everyone's anxious to meet you."

That was an understatement. As soon as she and Lance walked through the door, they were descended upon by an energetic group. In all the hugging, kissing, laughing and confusion of several people talking at one time, Jordan could hardly remember her own name, much less all the ones that were thrust at her. It was like old-home week. Besides Lance's immediate family, there were aunts, uncles, cousins and even a grandmother thrown in for good measure. Jordan gave up trying to keep them all straight, deciding she'd sort out everyone's name later.

But even amidst the confusion and disorder, she decided she liked Lance's family. His sister Abby, a tall, slim woman with dark curly hair and a sweet smile, was much like Clint, open and friendly. She welcomed Jordan like a long-lost sister, after first treating Lance to an exuberant hug and a smacking kiss. Her husband, whose name escaped Jordan, was of a quieter nature, but his smile had been genuine and his handshake strong.

Jordan had been especially nervous about meeting Lance's parents, afraid of what they'd read into the visit, but she soon found she need not have worried, at least not where his mother was concerned. Dorothy Rutledge was small and ageless. She could easily have passed for Abby's older sister. She greeted Jordan warmly, and there were tears in her eyes when she hugged her son.

"Oh, Lawrence, it's so good to have you home again," his mother said as she kissed his cheek, and Jordan met his gaze above his mother's head.

"Lawrence?" she mouthed in amazement.

His answer was a rueful grin and a slight shrug.

The only real surprise of the day was Lance's father. Abby had just ushered everyone out to the back patio for a buffet luncheon, when Matthew Rutledge walked in. Jordan would have recognized him anywhere. The resemblance between father and son was amazing, yet his greeting to Lance was cool, almost formal.

"Lance," the older man said, and the two men shook hands briefly.

"Sir," Lance responded, and Jordan could hear the tension in his voice.

"It's good of you to take time from your busy schedule to visit us . . . after all this time." His father's tone was harsh. "But I guess it's too much to expect a celebrity to remember he still has parents."

"Matthew!" Lines of distress creased her face as Dorothy quickly laid her hand on her husband's arm. "You promised!"

"So I did," he acknowledged, but his tone was bitter. "My apologies, Lance. To you and to your guest. We're pleased to have both of you. Now, if you'll excuse me, I have some things to attend to."

Lance stepped aside as his father brushed past him and opened the door. Matthew paused for a moment, his hand on the doorknob, and then he turned to his son. They stared at each other across the small distance until Matthew pulled open the door and stepped outside.

The moment the door closed, Lance's mother seemed to wilt. "Lawrence, I'm so sorry. I never meant for this to happen. I know your visit will be short and I was so hoping that the two of you would get along this time."

Lance's voice was soothing as he patted her hand. "Don't worry about it, mother. Things will work out."

Abby, coming back from the patio, chose that moment to interrupt. "Hey, gang, lunch is waiting! You better come and get it."

"Okay, we're coming," Lance said, and took Jordan's arm. "Go ahead, mother. Jordan and I will be there in a moment."

"All right, son. I'll save a place for you."

As soon as they were alone, Jordan gave way to her curiosity. "Lance, your father—"

He laid his finger across her lips. "Sshh. We'll talk about it later. Right now I'm starving. Let's go see what they have to eat."

They walked to the patio door before Jordan thought of her other question. "Lawrence?"

He grinned. "Matthew Lawrence Rutledge III," he said and pushed her through the patio door. "Now forget you ever heard it."

Lance was the center of attention at a table of older women, including his mother and grandmother. Jordan watched him as he bent his dark head toward his grandmother to catch something she was saying and saw the affectionate smile he gave her.

"He's really something," Abby said, following her gaze. "But then, he always was, even when we were kids. I was always so jealous of him. There didn't seem to be anything he couldn't do."

Jordan smiled. "Including ranching?"

"Especially ranching. It all seemed to come so natural to him." Abby paused, and when she continued her voice held a wistful note. "But then so did dreaming."

Her words halted Jordan's movements, and she held her fork suspended in midair. "Dreaming?"

"Oh, yeah. He was always somewhere else in his mind. I think that's one of the things that irritated dad the most. He used to say he never knew where Lance was even when he was looking at him." Abby smiled as she stirred sugar into her iced tea and took a sip. "When Lance got older, it really did get hard to find him. He'd slip away to the old movie house in town or be holed up somewhere with a pencil and a notebook, writing stories. We all figured he'd be a writer someday. All of us but dad, that is. He couldn't believe it when Lance went to California after his hitch in the Army instead of coming home. He'd always planned on turning the ranch over to Lance someday."

That could explain the antagonism she'd witnessed earlier, Jordan mused. "I thought Clint took care of the ranch."

"He does now," Abby answered. "Dad has a heart condition and is limited in what he can do. When it became evident that Lance wasn't coming home, he had no alternative but to turn it over to Clint."

Jordan buttered a slice of bread, trying to digest all of Abby's words. "You sound as though that's a problem."

"In a way." Abby said thoughtfully. "Clint, I'm afraid, is not the natural Lance was, and Dad dogs his footsteps day and night."

At least I stay and take it, Clint had said, and Jordan thought his statement made sense now. She thought again of the scene she had witnessed between Lance and his father and, remembering her own uneasy family situation, felt a surge of sympathy for the participants in this family drama. Dorothy, as wife and mother, was cast in the role of peacemaker, while Clint was the younger son who didn't quite measure up, and Lance was the prodigal son, punished for wanting to follow his own way.

Abby, seeing the expression of pain on Jordan's face, patted her arm comfortingly. "I'm sorry, Jordan. I didn't mean to burden you with our family problems. I guess you shouldn't be such a good listener."

"No, no. I'm glad you told me. You've answered a lot of questions for me."

"Lance seems very close to you. We were all surprised and thrilled"—she gestured around her—"as you can see, when Lance called last night to say he was coming today, but even more surprised when he said he was bringing you.

He hasn't brought anyone with him since Stephanie, and that was years ago."

At the mention of Lance's ex-wife, Jordan felt her interest rise, but purposely banked it down. If anyone told her about Stephanie Rutledge, she wanted it to be Lance. She decided it would be best if they changed the subject now, before it got too engrossing. She chose a safe topic, asking Abby about her husband and children and was relieved when that subject lasted through the rest of lunch.

9

The narrow, twisting trail had curved steadily upward for more than half an hour. Lance moved easily over the rough terrain with sure, economical motions that Jordan could only envy. Hot, sweaty and tired, she watched Lance's smooth progress as he climbed the path ahead of her, seemingly unmindful of the tall, thick grass that wrapped around her feet, the rocks that dug into the soles of her shoes or the hot Texas sun that beat relentlessly down on her bare head.

" 'Let's go for a walk,' " Jordan muttered, mimicking the invitation Lance had issued an hour earlier. "And stupid me said 'Sure, I love to walk.' Next time I'm going to ask for a map first."

She hated to admit to male superiority, but the truth was, this little trek was beginning to get to her. Halfway up the track, her legs began to wobble, causing her to lose her footing. As she scrambled for a handhold, she felt clumsy and awkward, and Lance's effortless pace irritated her greatly. How did he do it? She wasn't that much out of shape . . . was she?

Finally, chest heaving and muscles straining, she puffed to a stop beneath the branches of a massive old oak tree and yelled at his back. "Hey! I signed on for a walk, not an endurance test!"

Lance paused in mid-stride and looked over his shoulder at her, lifting his brows in amusement when he saw the sight she made slumped against the old tree, her hair disheveled, her clothes damp with perspiration and her chest heaving from exertion.

"Something wrong?"

"Lance, I'll admit to being a bit old-fashioned, but I think you have a lot to learn about going for a walk." She slid to the ground, her back still braced against the tree. "A 'walk' is normally accomplished at a nice, leisurely pace, in pleasant surroundings in a rather relaxed atmosphere. People usually amble along together and talk, look at the scenery, they can even hold hands"—why on earth had she said that?—"but one of the cardinal rules is never to try to annihilate one's walking partner."

"You're not enjoying the tour?" he asked with innocent concern.

"Foolish of me, I guess, but when you invited me to go for a walk, I envisioned a peaceful country lane or perhaps a treelined path. I'd even have settled for a cow track! You never said a word about running an obstacle course, dodging rattlesnake holes or climbing a mountain!"

Grinning, he retraced his steps, and Jordan noted with disgust that he wasn't even breathing hard. The least he could do, she fumed, was break into a shirt-drenching sweat.

"And I thought you were a country girl," he teased as he dropped down beside her on the tufted grass.

"You should have warned me and I would've brought my hiking boots and backpack."

Dark eyes gleamed wickedly. "The trail's not too tough for you, is it? I did offer to stay behind and help. Bring up the rear, so to speak."

She shot him a speaking glance, then let her gaze travel

upward over the rough, spiraling trail still ahead of them. "For your sake, I hope this leads somewhere. If it doesn't, you're in serious trouble."

"One of my favorite places is up there." He shrugged, his expression properly woeful. "I wanted you to see it. I figured that if anyone in the world would appreciate this place it would be you, but if it's going to be too much for you, I guess we should head back down."

Aware that she was playing into his hands, Jordan still could not resist the challenge. "That's okay, Lance. I appreciate your concern, but I came this far; I intend to see what's so fascinating at the top of this hill!"

He sprang easily to his feet and held out a hand to Jordan. "Come on then. We're almost there."

She groaned wearily, but took his hand. "Is this some kind of Texas torture?" she asked when she was standing beside him.

He kissed her lightly on the lips and whispered suggestively, "No, but remind me later, and I'll be happy to devise one for you."

Excitement raced like electrical current down her spine and, suddenly flustered, she tried to step away from him, but he retained his hold on her hand.

"I think I'd better hold on to this a while," he told her, tightening his grip. "The trail gets a little steep from here. Besides, wasn't it you who said that walking partners should hold hands?"

Somehow she'd known that remark would come back to haunt her, but she left her hand where it was.

He hadn't exaggerated. For the next twenty minutes, the climb was all but straight up. Jordan was soon hotter, wearier and more out of breath than before. All that kept her going was Lance's fingers intertwined with hers.

He glanced over his shoulder at her, and his gaze was gentle. "How are you doing?"

She tried not to pant. "Fine. I'm even beginning to enjoy this little expedition."

"Good. Just a little farther and we're there. Look." He pointed upward. "You can see it from here."

Her gaze followed the line of his finger and suddenly her breath stilled as she caught her first sight of their destination. It reminded her of an oasis in the desert, and suddenly she knew exactly where she was.

She had assumed they were headed for the top of the mountain, but realized now that their destination lay many feet below the crest on a natural shelf that cut into the side of the rock, creating a large, open-air cavern. Grass grew thick and lush in the opening, and a small pool just at the mouth of the shelter bubbled with fresh water from an underground spring. A heavy growth of underbrush hugged the cave walls and Jordan quickly decided she didn't want to venture too deep into the cavern.

He helped her up the last few steps to the ledge, then stood looking around him, pleasure and satisfaction lighting his face.

"This was your 'hole' when you were a kid, wasn't it?"

He glanced at her sharply. "How did you know that?"

She laughed at his expression as she dropped down beside the small pool and idly trailed her hand through the cool water. "Don't look so surprised. It wasn't hard to figure out. Abby told me that when you were a kid you had a habit of slipping off to the old movie house in town or holing up somewhere alone. I can't imagine a more perfect spot for 'holing up' than right here. It's really beautiful."

"It is, isn't it?" He wandered over to the pool. "I found it accidentally one day. I'd gotten into another scrape with dad and wanted to be alone to lick my wounds. I started walking and climbing just to work off my temper and frustration. I found this place instead and was positive God had created it just for me."

"Perhaps he did."

Lance smiled as though the thought amused him. "It's a nice thought, but this place was here a long time before me."

"I can picture you here as a boy," she said, glancing around her. "I can see you with your notebook and your pencil, writing stories and dreaming of cowboys and Indians."

He laughed. "You're a perceptive woman." He drew a deep breath and looked away. "I wish everyone understood me as well as you."

She realized that this was the opening she'd been waiting for. "Lance, tell me about your father."

He didn't answer immediately, but stood silently pondering the watery depths of the pool. Fearing that she had offended him by asking such a personal question, she hastily added, "Lance, I'm sorry. I shouldn't have—"

"No, it's okay," he interrupted. "I want to tell you about it. I was just wondering where to begin."

He dropped down beside her to the mossy bank. "I guess the best way to describe the relationship with my father is to describe the lack of one. I never understood him, he never understood me, and the result was constant friction. My mother always said the reason we couldn't get along was that we were too much alike."

Jordan smiled. She had thought Dorothy Rutledge a very astute woman the moment she'd met her.

"Anyway, I suppose he felt that because I was the oldest son, I should naturally follow in his footsteps. Unfortunately, I had plans of my own. I can't remember a time when I didn't want to write. And after I discovered movies, well, the two just seemed to go hand in hand."

"But he should have been proud of your talent." She couldn't prevent the protest.

Lance shook his head. "I'm afraid to my father it was all just so much nonsense, something to occupy time that could have been spent doing something worthwhile."

"Abby told me you were good at ranching. Surely that pleased him."

"Oh, yeah. That pleased him. Unfortunately, that was one

of the reasons he couldn't understand my wasting time doing anything else. So this"—he gestured around him—"was my escape. I'd pack up some grub, as I called it back then, roll up my sleeping bag, better known in those days as a bedroll, fill my canteen with soda pop and slip up here to stay as long as I thought I could before they sent out a search party."

"And when you went home?"

"I'd catch hell! I always knew I would, but it was worth it at the time."

Sympathy stirred in her breast for the young Lance. "Did you ever try talking to him? Explain to him how you felt about your writing?"

"Only about a million times." He lifted her hand, idly running his fingers over hers. "I'm afraid my dad is not the easiest of men to reason with. He tends to see things only one way."

In unison, they said, "His way," then looked at each other and laughed.

"You seem well acquainted with the man," Lance said when he'd recovered.

"No, just someone very similar." She hesitated before adding, "My own father, as a matter of fact." It surprised her to hear a wistful note in her voice. Did it still matter so much, after all these years? "It's ironic that neither of us was the son our fathers wanted."

Lance remembered the father she'd described in *A Private War* and struggled to keep the surprise from his face. This was the closest she'd ever come to opening up to him and he was suddenly afraid to say anything, afraid the fragile moment would be shattered. He chose his words with care. "Do I take it that your father was disappointed in you because you were female instead of male?"

She nodded. "I'm afraid our troubles began the day I was born and went downhill from there. I was his last chance at a boy, and needless to say, I blew it. I don't think he ever forgave my mother or me. That's how I ended up with the name Jordan. He'd chosen it for his son, but when I came along instead, he decided to use it anyway." She gave a soft laugh. "I guess I should be thankful; I could have been a Ralph or an Irving. Jordan's not half-bad when you consider the alternatives."

Lance leaned over and kissed the tip of her nose. "You're the most beautiful Jordan I've ever known. Besides, it suits you. You're not the Mary Jane or Betty Jo type."

"Thank you . . . I think." She was silent for a moment, then she said quietly, "I don't mind the name, really, I just wish my father and I could have had some sort of relationship."

"I know what you mean," Lance said gently. "I always felt that I was missing something. Something important. I guess, secretly, I always wanted his approval, but we could never seem to find any common ground. And because we couldn't, it put a strain on the whole family, my mother especially. Her son on one side, her husband on the other. That's why I left home as early as I could. I figured everyone would be better off without me around causing friction."

It sounded strange, all her mixed and sometimes contradictory emotions about her family, being put into words by someone else, but Lance had summed up her feelings quite accurately while describing his own situation. Somehow, it was comforting to know that she wasn't the only one who had flunked Family Relationships 101 and, judging by the scene she had witnessed earlier, Lance and his father were not making great strides toward improving their dealings with each other.

"You've never been able to reconcile your differences, even now that you're older?" she asked cautiously.

"No, in fact, sometimes I think the gap gets wider instead of narrower. My father feels I let him down when he was forced to retire and I wasn't here to take over the ranch." He focused his attention on her hand, which he still held in his.

"How about you? Did getting older and leaving home solve things?"

"I'm afraid not." She smiled, but the smile was tinged with sadness. "As I told you before, I divorced their hand-picked son-in-law. I'm afraid that didn't do much for my image. As far as my father was concerned, I blew my only chance to redeem myself."

Confession hour suddenly became too much for her and she got to her feet, squinting up at the sun as she rose. "Shouldn't we be heading back? It looks as though it's getting late."

Lance, always sensitive to her moods, smiled at her equivocation, but followed without protest. He'd always known that talking about her past made her nervous, and she'd given enough for one day. He had no desire to shatter the fragile peace existing between them.

He glanced at the slim watch circling his wrist. "Dinner should be ready by the time we get back." He cupped a hand around his ear as though listening to a distant call. "Yep. Just as I thought. Cook's biscuits and gravy are calling."

"You idiot!" She poked a finger at his ribs, but he caught her hand and secured it in his. She regarded their laced fingers for a moment before lifting her eyes to his. "Thank you for bringing me today, not only to see this—and it really was worth the climb—but also to meet your family and see your home. You were right, we needed a break."

He gave her hand a gentle squeeze. "It's been nice, hasn't it? Almost twenty-four hours without an argument." He studied her face for a moment, and when he spoke, his voice was without its normal humor. "Jordan, I hope you under-stand about the script; I'm really not trying to butcher your book. I want this movie to be great, as you do, but I also know what it takes to make a good, workable screenplay."

She was glad for the truce. She didn't take time to question why; she merely reached for it, eagerly. "I realize that, Lance, and I should be the one apologizing. I seem to be the one starting all the arguments lately. I don't know why—"

He stopped her with a finger against her lips. "You don't have to apologize. Not to me. I know how important it is to you. I just want you to understand that I'll do all I can to insure that your story is transferred to film as accurately and sensitively as possible."

His words humbled her and she was suddenly ashamed of her lack of faith. "I know that, Lance. I guess down deep I've always known it. That's why I feel so ashamed now. I . . ." She looked away from him. "I never wanted anyone but you to write the script. Somehow I always knew you'd do the best job." She grimaced as she turned back to face him. "I know that sounds strange coming from the person who's done nothing but plague you day and night—"

"You certainly have done that, although not necessarily over the script." He smiled as she blushed, then became serious as another thought occurred. "Have you talked to that agent of yours lately?"

"Ryan?" She drew out the name, wondering at the sudden shift in conversation. "No. Should I have?"

"I called Durrell last night to tell him we'd be away for a few days, and he mentioned that he was negotiating with Collier for the film rights to another one of your books. He asked if I'd be interested in writing the screenplay."

She considered that information for a moment before answering, *"Paper Dolls,* I suppose."

Lance nodded. "You knew about it?"

"Ryan told me Durrell had expressed an interest in the film rights, but I haven't heard any specifics on an offer yet." Tension tightened her throat as she inquired, "What did you tell Durrell?"

"That it was up to you." He watched for her reaction. "That I wouldn't do anything without your approval."

"My approval?" she repeated, incredulous. "Why did you tell him that?"

He laid his hands gently on her shoulders. "Jordan, I

understand how important your books are to you. I know how much time and effort and hard work goes into each one. I've watched you working on this script and that new book of yours and I'm constantly amazed by your drive and persistence and dedication to detail." He grinned wryly. "Now I know why I write screenplays and not novels."

"That still doesn't explain why you need my approval to write a screenplay," Jordan insisted.

He shrugged and let his hands slide down her arms to her wrists, before joining his hands with hers. "I know you've been less than thrilled with the way I've handled *A Private War*. I wouldn't blame you if you didn't want me involved in another project."

She shook her head vigorously. "Don't be ridiculous, Lance. You're . . . you're the best screenwriter in Hollywood. I'm honored you would even consider doing another adaptation of one of my books, especially since I've been such a pain to work with on this one."

Again, he laid his finger across her lips. "Sssh. I won't have you talking that way about the woman I love."

"Oh, Lance, how can you say things like that? You know what an idiot I am. I'm—"

"—kind and caring, beautiful and intelligent," he finished for her. "I know. I also know you're sweet and sensitive and sexy as hell."

"No, I'm not," she began in protest, but his lips settled over hers, silencing her objection.

"You do like to argue," he murmured when he lifted his head.

"You bring it on yourself," she told him, breathless from his kiss but not wanting to admit that such a casual embrace could stir such a reaction. "You deliberately say things to confuse or provoke me."

He grinned, totally unrepentant. "You're right. I keep hoping someday you'll forget to say no, and say yes for a change."

She pushed playfully at his chest. "I knew you had an ulterior motive."

"But is it working?" he demanded, the gleam in his eye belying the gloom in his voice.

He took one final look around his childhood retreat before leading her to the edge of the mountainside clearing and back to the path they had climbed earlier. "Come on. We'd better get back to the house. Mom will have a fit if we're late for dinner."

"I'll tell her it was all your fault," Jordan said as she took the first step down the vertical path.

Dawn was just beginning to creep over the eastern horizon when Lance banged on her door the next morning. She rolled away from the sound and tried to bury her head under a pillow, but the racket continued until, with a whispered oath, she staggered from the bed and fumbled her way to the door. The moment she pulled it open, she became uncomfortably aware of her early morning dishabille.

"Lance!" she hissed, tugging at the hem of her thigh-length nightshirt. "What's wrong with you? Don't you know what time it is?"

His gaze roamed over her appreciatively. "The question is, do *you* know what time it is? Last night you said you wanted to go with Clint and me to see how a ranch really operated. Well, this is operation rule number one—breakfast at five-thirty, on the job by six."

"Ugh," was her succinct reply.

He leaned a shoulder against the doorframe. "If it's too early for you, we'll be back by lunch. I'm sure Mom wouldn't mind the company."

Another one of those sneaky challenges of his, she thought, recognizing his tone and knowing she couldn't let it pass. "Thanks anyway, but I'm awake now. No use in wasting the morning."

"Good. I'll see you downstairs in five minutes."

Five minutes! she mouthed, watching him disappear down the hallway. She couldn't wash the sleep from her eyes in five minutes! But she did want to see the rest of the ranch and Lance had offered to show it to her. Suddenly the day seemed brighter. She hurried to the bathroom, grabbing the jeans and shirt she'd laid out the night before. Today would be another day to spend with Lance, a whole day of learning and enjoying, without the shadow of the script to come between them.

Lance and Clint were seated at the dining room table when Jordan hurried in ten minutes later, and Lance made a show of consulting his watch as she pulled out a chair and dropped down beside him.

"Not too bad," he murmured, his gaze seductive, and Jordan was left wondering if his comment referred to her speedy arrival or her appearance in general.

"I hope I didn't keep you waiting," she said, noting the clean, empty plates in front of them.

"Naw," Clint said, reaching for the coffee keeper. "Cook said breakfast wouldn't be ready for another five minutes or so. Would you like some coffee while you wait?"

"Why, you scoundrel!" Jordan exclaimed, turning on Lance. "You tricked me."

"How else was I going to get a dawdling female ready in fifteen minutes?" he asked.

After breakfast was finally served and consumed, Jordan followed the men outside to the barn, coming to an abrupt halt when she saw three horses, saddled and waiting, standing by the fence.

"Oh, no. Oh, no." She began to backpedal, intending to put as much distance as possible between herself and the huge animals, but Lance reached out and snagged her wrist, preventing her escape.

"Hey, I thought you wanted to see the place," he said, maintaining a firm grip when she would have pulled away.

"I do, but not if that's the only transportation."

"We're going to check on a herd over in the east pasture. The easiest way to get there is on horseback. Surely, you've ridden a horse before?" His gaze took in her flushed face and wide-eyed stare. "You've never been on a horse before?"

"You don't have to say it as though I missed some vital part of my education," Jordan snapped. "Not everyone is from Texas, you know."

"Okay, I'm sorry. I wasn't trying to be smart. Perhaps I should rephrase my question. Would you like to try horseback riding? It's the best way to really see the land, and I think you would enjoy it once you got the hang of it."

She smiled in spite of herself. "Funny you should put it like that. I was just picturing something very similar—me, hanging on for dear life."

Lance smiled, but when he answered, his voice was serious. "You know I wouldn't let anything hurt you. If you want to give it a try, I'll show you the basics and I think you'll catch on with no trouble. But if you'd rather not, we'll take the pickup and I'll show you what I can of the place from the truck."

Had he always been this sneaky, she wondered.

"All right. I'll try it," she heard herself saying a moment later. "But I want you to understand that my life is in your hands."

The look he gave her could have melted cold steel, and Jordan's all-too-human bones stood no chance at all. "I wondered how long it would be before you realized that," he told her.

An hour later, mounted on a sedate little mare called Mandy, Jordan followed Lance into an immense open pasture and watched with a mingling of pride and envy the ease and grace he displayed in the saddle. While she struggled just to stay astride, he sat tall and erect, moving with his mount as if they were one.

They hadn't gone far when Lance slowed his pace and dropped back to ride along beside her. "How's it going, Annie Oakley?"

"I'm fine," she said, shifting slightly in the saddle. "It's my rump that has the problem."

He grinned. "Try sitting farther back in the saddle so that you don't get the motion of both the front and back legs of the horse," he instructed. "Remember what I told you. Don't move against the motion. Ride with it."

"That's easier said than done," she said a moment later after trying to do as he said. "I keep sliding forward, then I start bouncing again."

"That means the saddle is too big for you or the stirrups are too long." He sent an appraising glance over her. "Don't worry, we're almost there. You can get down and rest your . . . legs."

They met Clint about five minutes later just as he was closing the gate on the east pasture. "I was about to give up on you two," he told them as they reined in beside him.

"Had to give some riding lessons," Lance said, stepping down from the tall bay he rode. Moving to her side, he lifted Jordan from her saddle, holding her firmly while she tried out her legs again. "Can you walk?" he asked gently.

Reluctantly, she stepped away from him. "Better than I ride, obviously."

"You did fine for your first time out. I'm proud of you." He took her hand and pulled her into step beside him. "Come on, Annie. We'll walk for a while so you can work some of the kinks out of your muscles."

They ended up walking most of the way back, not remounting until they were less than a mile from the house. She handled the horse much better the second time and earned not only Lance's approval, but Clint's as well. She flushed under their praise and was beginning to think she was born and bred for ranch life.

This belief was further reinforced when she discovered that she possessed a natural dexterity with a lariat. Clint had three small calves in a separate holding pen, awaiting innoculations. She watched the brothers rope and tie each calf, holding it steady until the proper shots had been given. After the calves were released, the two men began arguing about who was the better roper, and Jordan was even invited to try her hand. After receiving instructions on how to hold and throw the rough-textured braid, she was pleasantly surprised when after a few initial tries, the rope began to settle with growing accuracy over the practice target. But it wasn't until she tried to snare a live target that she realized there was more to the feat than skill with a rope.

Despite Lance's warnings, she threw her loop over one of the small calves still wandering around in the pen. She was delighted, yet amazed, when it settled over the calf's neck in an almost perfect throw. She was more amazed when the calf started in a dead run for the opposite end of the pen with her dangling on the end of her own rope.

Lance was instantly beside her, picking her up and dusting her off and trying very hard to conceal the smile that tugged at the corners of his mouth.

"Are you all right?" he asked solicitously.

More embarrassed than injured, she pulled out of his grasp and began her own dusting and straightening procedure. "I'm fine," she informed him for the second time that morning, and watched as he ducked his face from her view. "If you dare laugh, Lance Rutledge," she warned severely, then made the mistake of meeting his eyes as he lifted his gaze back to hers. There was an irresistible twinkle in the amber depths and, before she could prevent herself, she responded to it. They collapsed against each other, laughing until tears ran down their faces. Clint, watching from the sidelines, could only shake his head in wonder.

The next order of business involved unloading a truckload of alfalfa hay, and as soon as lunch was finished, the two brothers tackled the job, with Clint on the trailer tossing bales down, and Lance on the ground, restacking them in the barn. Jordan quickly gave up the notion of helping when she realized that one bale weighed almost as much as she did.

It was fascinating to watch Lance in these new and unfamiliar surroundings. Since they'd met, she'd seen Lance in many different settings. She remembered how smooth and polished he had seemed that first night in the restaurant, how casually he'd worn his tailored suit and silk shirt. She could picture him standing on her porch in his immaculately creased jeans and spit-shined boots, the early morning sun creating golden highlights in his hair. And she could see him barefoot and barechested, propped against her couch watching the late, late movie on TV.

There were other mental photographs she could call to mind with equal ease. Lance behind his typewriter, serious and dignified. Lance in the kitchen, hopping between the pan on the stove and the one in the oven. Lance relaxed and romantic, staring into her eyes with the flicker of firelight lighting his own.

Today had given her a whole new set of photographs to add to her collection. Lance on horseback, tall and proud. Lance playing vet, a rope in one hand, a syringe in the other. And Lance stripped to the waist, his chest slicked and gleaming with sweat, tossing eighty-pound bales of hay around as though he did it every day.

Jordan leaned back against the tailgate of the pickup with sudden weakness. A realization swept over her with such strength and clarity that she shivered under its force. How could she have been so blind? Yet this was not a sudden revelation. She should have seen it coming weeks ago. She should have recognized the signs, realized what was happening, but she'd been so stubbornly arrogant in her belief that she was immune, she had refused to see what was right before her eyes.

She was in love with Lance Rutledge.

Timeless moments passed as she sat dazed, disoriented, totally engrossed in her new discovery. When Lance's voice finally penetrated the fog that shrouded her mind, she gazed at him wonderingly. He must have seen something in her expression, because he immediately dropped the bale of hay he'd been carrying and came to her side.

"Are you all right?"

She blinked and her vision cleared, allowing her to see him as she should have seen him weeks before. The smile she gave him was tremulous. "I'm fine," she said for the third time that day. "Just fine."

10

Lance watched her idly toss pebbles into the lapping waters. Something was bothering her. It was obvious in the set of her shoulders and the silence she wore around her like a protective veil.

It frustrated him to see the fear and confusion return to her face, especially when she'd been so cheerful and carefree only hours earlier. Jordan had never been an easy person to understand, but today's transition was more baffling than usual.

When he'd first noticed the changes in her earlier in the afternoon, he'd thought perhaps she was experiencing a delayed reaction to the tumble she'd taken, but she'd assured him that physically she was fine. He'd sent her back to the house anyway, with instructions to soak in a hot tub and to lie down and rest. She'd done both, but when she had come back downstairs, she had appeared as nervous and troubled as before.

So he had risked his mother's disfavor by wheedling his

way out of her dinner plans, and he had brought Jordan to
this lakeside setting for an impromptu picnic, hoping that the
combination of peaceful water and shimmering moonlight
would be enough to erase the haunted, hunted look from
her eyes.

She'd said very little since their arrival at the small private
lake and it hurt to know that she didn't trust him enough to
confide in him. But from the beginning, he had promised
Jordan and himself that he'd be patient. He had promised
not to demand, rush or pressure. He chafed now under the
bonds of that pledge, knowing that to break it would be to
lose her for good.

Restlessly, he moved to stand beside her at the water's
edge, watching her listless movements as she tossed in
another small stone. She watched the ripples circle and
dissolve, then cast another in its wake.

"Momentous thoughts call for momentous actions," he
observed wryly when she gave no sign of acknowledging his
presence.

Another pebble landed with a small splash. "I'm in a
momentous mood," she answered.

"You want to tell me about it?"

"That depends." She continued throwing rocks in the
water. "You may not want to hear it."

Lance stiffened and raw pain tore through his chest. Was
this it? Was she going to tell him what he'd feared since the
beginning? He opened his mouth to speak, then closed it,
afraid to trust his voice. He hadn't realized he was so
vulnerable.

Carefully, he cleared his throat and tried again. "Why
don't you try me? I might surprise you."

"All right." She turned to face him. "I was wondering
about your marriage. About your ex-wife."

If she'd hit him with a baseball bat, she couldn't have
surprised him more. He stared at her for several seconds
before finding his voice to inquire disbelievingly, "My
what?"

"See? I warned you. I was afraid you wouldn't want to hear it." Her tone was flat, dejected.

"No, no. It's not that," he said quickly. "You took me by surprise, that's all." He took a deep breath. "What do you want to know?"

She glanced away from him. "Everything, I guess. How did you meet? How long were you married? What was she like? Why did you divorce?" She swung back to him, and he could see the hesitation and determination in her face. "I remember you telling me that the two of you weren't going in the same direction, but now that I know you better, I find it hard to believe that you would forfeit your marriage for such a . . . a flimsy reason. I think that, for you at least, it would have had to be something major—something unforgivable—for you to have even considered divorce."

She looked away again. "You don't have to tell me any of these things; there's really no reason why you should. I know I have a nerve to even ask, and I'll accept that it's none of my business if you'd prefer not to talk about it. But"—her voice dropped to a thin thread of sound—"I would like to know."

He cradled her face in his hands, gazing deeply into the troubled depths of her eyes. "Don't you know by now that you can ask me anything? I'll tell you anything; I'll do anything as long as it makes you happy."

The blanket where they'd spread their picnic was only a few steps behind them, and Lance drew her down with him, their bodies close, touching, as they settled together to the ground.

"Actually, I'm glad you asked about Stephanie," he began a moment later, aware of the effort it had cost her to ask. "I've never told anyone else the whole story." He plucked a blade of grass and twirled it between his fingers.

"We met through the studio. She was an aspiring young actress, and I had just completed my first feature film. I was feeling cocky and self-assured, and she must have been impressed. We dated for a while, but it wasn't until after my 'sleeper' film hit big at the box office that she and I began to get serious. At the time, it never occurred to me to question the timing of our relationship. I knew she was ambitious, but who wasn't?

"For a time it seemed that absolutely nothing could go wrong in my life. I was promoted to senior writer on the television series I'd been working on, and for the first time since the show's inception, it edged its way into the top ten in the ratings. The producer loved me and began lining up outside projects for me. My second feature did well at the box office and it seemed that my career was set. Meanwhile, Stephanie's hadn't been doing so well. Small roles, walk-ons, commercials, were about all she'd been able to get. Male chauvinist that I was, I didn't give it too much thought.

"I still didn't, even after she agreed to marry me. I had asked her before, but she'd always said no, maintaining that it would be bad for her image as a screen personality. It never occurred to me she thought marriage to me could boost her career." He drew a ragged breath. "She had me fooled all the way. I couldn't understand why other people didn't seem as enamored of her as I was. I guess the bottom line was that I wanted to be in love. I wanted to be married. I'd always looked forward to having a family of my own, and I guess I thought I'd finally have what I'd always wanted. But we were young and just starting our careers, and Stephanie persuaded me to wait to start a family. I had no idea that she didn't want one at all."

Lance's voice roughened as he continued. "We'd been married a little over two years when Stephanie found out she was pregnant. I was delighted, but she was furious. She'd just landed a small part in an important film, and she claimed that being pregnant would ruin it for her. I knew she was upset, but I didn't think too much about it. I figured when she had time to get used to the idea, she'd be as happy about it as I was."

Jordan's stomach tightened as she waited for him to continue. He stared into the distance for several seconds before continuing in a voice that was tight with strain.

"It wasn't until later I learned that she had no intention of 'getting used to it.' About two weeks after the pregnancy was confirmed, I came home to find her propped up in bed—recuperating. I asked her what was wrong and she told me she'd been to the doctor and had the 'problem' taken care of."

His grip on Jordan's hand tightened, painfully, as he turned to stare into her face. Even in the dim glow of midnight, she could see his expression, stark and unforgiving, and shuddered for the woman who had been foolish enough to tempt this man's hatred.

"She'd had an abortion!" Lance continued in a low voice. "Without telling me, without giving me a chance to have any say in the decision, she terminated her pregnancy and killed our child."

"Oh, Lance." Her eyes filled with tears for him. She knew how much he'd suffered. "I'm so sorry. I had no idea."

"No one did. I couldn't bring myself to tell anyone. Not even my family. It's difficult to admit you've been a fool. I had married an image, an illusion. She told me later that she'd never loved me. I seriously doubt she could ever love anyone but herself, but that part didn't bother me. I just couldn't believe she could destroy our child without a single regret." His hand balled into a fist. "You can't know how I hated her at that moment! It was all I could do to get out of that apartment without doing something violent."

Gently, Jordan laid her other hand across the one that held hers in its punishing grip. She didn't try to break the grip. Instinctively, she knew he needed something warm to hold on to.

She made her decision without being aware that there was a decision to be made.

"Lance," she said, and her voice was soft, "I do know." She paused and the moment was electric. "I know because I too lost a child. I lost my baby in the front seat of a car on a lonely stretch of highway eight years ago. I lost it because of another person's selfishness and cruelty." Her voice cracked slightly. "And I know what it's like to want to respond to violence with violence—but we're not the violent kind."

His eyes were suddenly very dark. He made no pretense of misunderstanding what she was saying. And though there was joy that she'd finally opened up to him, there was pain that had to be dealt with first. "Yes, you do know. You know about all of it, don't you?"

"I know about losing," she said in a voice he hardly recognized. "I know about disappointment. I know about pain so strong you don't think you can possibly live through it. And I know about hate so consuming that it gives you a will to live and go on when nothing else can."

"Rachel?" Now that she had opened up, he wanted it all out.

"Yes." A low sigh escaped her. "No one else ever suspected that that book was even partially autobiographical. Not even Ryan. You floored me that first night when you said no one could know Rachel better than Rachel. But basically, you were right. I changed a few facts to make the story flow smoothly and to incorporate some of my research, but the overall story is mine. How did you know?"

"I always told you I understood more than you gave me credit for," he answered gently. "I suppose the reason I did was because of the many parallels in our lives. You weren't the son your father wanted, and while I was of the correct gender, I was never the son my father wanted either. We both ended up in bad marriages and we both lost children we shouldn't have lost. We had a lifetime in common before we ever met."

"I'm sorry that I lied to you about Rachel. It wasn't that I wanted to. I just couldn't bear another person's pity, or worse, their condemnation."

"Why would I condemn you? You were the victim, for God's sake!"

"Many people didn't see it that way, unfortunately. Including my parents. Philip made certain that no one ever saw his dark side except me. To the rest of the world, he was a loving, dedicated, hard-working husband, and I was the cross he had to bear. It was a convincing image, and he worked hard to maintain it. He never let anyone else see the man who could fly into a black rage just because a shirt wasn't pressed to suit him or dinner was late."

"Why did you stay and take it? Why didn't you get out?" Lance had intended to remain silent, but the words exploded from him before he could prevent them.

"That's always the first question," Jordan said, with a mirthless laugh. "It seems so obvious to everyone that I should have packed my bags and walked away. I wish it had been that simple, but Philip controlled everything—my time, my friends, our finances. Where do you go when you have no car, no money, and no one to turn to?"

"But surely your parents would have helped you."

She shook her head. "I married Philip to please my father. Philip's family owned one of the largest construction companies in Denver. My father was in building supply. You can see why he thought it was a match made in heaven. There was no way he would have done anything to offend a Winslow."

Lance made an angry movement beside her. "The only time I went to my parents for help, my father told me I must have provoked Philip and gave me a thirty-minute lecture on what a recalcitrant child I had been and said that it was obvious I hadn't changed. He told me how lucky I was to have Philip Winslow for a husband, then he took me home and apologized to Philip."

She gave another laugh that was but a harsh thread of sound and fought to keep her tears at bay. "Can you imagine? He apologized to Philip!" There was silence for a moment as she struggled for control, and when she spoke again, her voice trembled just above a whisper. "I tried talking to my minister once, but he believed very strongly in the sanctity of marriage, and his only advice was for me to be a good wife and make the best of the situation. After that, I never asked anyone for help. I did try to make the best of things and go on—until I found out I was pregnant. Then I had more than just myself to worry about. I had the responsibility for my child."

She turned to stare out across the narrow expanse of water, and her shoulders slumped. "You know the rest of the story. I made plans to leave. I saved money from my household allowance, sold my few good pieces of jewelry and bought a one-way ticket out of Denver. But Philip found the suitcase I'd hidden in a closet." She gulped back a sob as simultaneous waves of grief and regret washed over her. "I thought I was protecting my baby, but I ended up killing it instead."

Her tears would no longer be contained and, as Lance pulled her into his arms, pressing her trembling body into the warmth and strength of his own, she began to weep passionately, giving release to the pent-up pain and frustration she'd carried with her for too many years.

"Let it go," Lance murmured, burying his face in her hair. "You don't have to be so strong. You've got me now. I'll take care of you."

He continued to hold her, lulling her with his soothing words, and she let herself relax against him. She felt as though a heavy yoke had been lifted from her shoulders. Even her tears had been cleansing, and she realized that it was the first time she had ever cried for herself.

"I've been a fool, haven't I?" she murmured when at last she could speak again. "I don't see how you can stand to put up with me. I've acted like an idiot, lied to you, and been such a coward I couldn't admit I wanted you."

"Do you want me?" The question shimmered between them and Lance held his breath waiting for her reply.

She lifted her hands to his face and a swell of emotion surged through him at her touch.

"Yes," she answered, suddenly shy. "Yes, I want you very much."

He stared down at her for a moment, then his lips closed over hers in a kiss that was at once passion and tenderness, promise and demand. She had no choice but to respond. All her defenses had been shattered. There were no longer any barriers Lance couldn't breach. But with his mouth doing such wonderful things to hers, she found that she no longer cared.

She burrowed closer to the delicious warmth of his body and felt his arms tighten around her.

"Show me," he whispered against her lips. "Show me that you want me."

Jordan smiled at his request. He'd been in charge of pursuit since the beginning; it was only fair that she take her turn.

In one fluid motion, she rolled to her knees and placed her arms around his neck. She held his face pressed against her breasts for a long moment, before drawing back to gaze tenderly down into his face. Her hands slid slowly forward until her palms cupped his face between them, and with the merest whisper of a touch, she placed her lips against his mouth. He remained still and passive within her embrace, and though he didn't resist, neither did he respond. She knew he was waiting for a sign of commitment. He would have it.

She let her tongue and lips play over his, teasing the corner of his mouth, nibbling at the tender fullness of his bottom lip, sliding her tongue across his teeth. When that achieved only limited response—his breath had quickened —she moved closer, letting her breasts brush lightly against his chest. There was a definite intake of breath then, perhaps a tightening of muscle, but no other reaction.

Using her teeth and her tongue, she mapped a moist trail across his jawline to the sensitive area just below his ear. A tremor shook his body and gave her the courage to place her lips against his ear.

"Love me, Lance. I need you." Her voice was a shadowy whisper in the darkness. "Make love to me . . . please."

Tenderly, lovingly, he gathered her into his arms, pulling her down on his lap. "Jordan." His voice trembled. "My God, I've waited so long to hear you say that. I'd given up hope."

"So had I," she said, her thoughts on the years she'd believed there could be no love for her. But she'd been given a new beginning. A new chance. She had no intention of losing a second time. She lifted her face to him in silent offering. "Love me tonight," she whispered.

He needed no second bidding. Lowering his head, he claimed her lips in a sweet, drugging kiss that had no boundaries in time, only roots in eternity. A kiss that expressed more than need and hunger and passion. A kiss that promised love and trust and honesty. And at that moment, it was all they needed.

But as that moment passed, other needs became more pressing. The need to know and share each other—completely. The need to give pleasure and peace to each other—completely. The need to heal each other—completely. Soon they were clinging to each other, and the barriers between them broke, the walls between them tumbled.

Lance pulled her to the ground with him. The soft padding of late summer grass was there to cushion their bodies and, as Jordan settled on her back, Lance was there above her, his lips gently caressing her ear, her neck and her throat until she could think of nothing but having those lips on hers. His mouth hovered over hers, almost touching. He watched her for a moment, until a small groan of frustration escaped her and, with a teasing smile, he brought his lips down to meet hers. Her arms fastened around his neck, and she pressed herself against him, instantly feeling the surge of passion in his body, and the answering ache of her own.

He tugged at the hem of her blouse, loosening it from the

waistband of her jeans, and slipped his hand inside the material to stroke and caress her bare skin. Her gasp echoed through the night as his palm closed over the taut fullness of her breast, and she arched into his hand.

Liquid fire raced through her veins as his lips touched upon her again, finding the responsive areas of her throat and neck. The ache she had begun to feel spread and intensified as his mouth continued its journey, seeking and closing upon the swollen and hard-tipped peak of her breast. He nursed her gently through the soft fabric of her blouse.

When he lifted his head, his eyes locked with hers and his words were soft as he whispered, "I want to see you, Jordan. I want to see all of you."

His gaze remained on her face as his hand went to the top button of her blouse, then the second, then the third. In a matter of seconds, all the buttons were released and he was pushing the cloth from her shoulders. Her lacy bra was next to go and, as he tossed it aside, he bent over her, taking her greedily into his mouth. A thousand tiny explosions followed.

His hands quickly dispensed with the fastening on her jeans, and the metallic rasp of her zipper sounded loudly into the night. He tugged them downward over her hips, and for a moment, she resisted, suddenly unsure of the course she'd set out to follow.

Lance stilled his movements, recognizing her uncertainty. "Sshh, sweetheart. I only want to love you."

Gathering her courage, she put her deepest fears into words. "It's been so long, Lance. What if I can't please you? I'm not very experienced at this. What if I disappoint you?"

He cradled her to him, and his lips touched hers gently. "You can't disappoint me. Just being with you pleases me. Holding you pleases me." His voice dropped to a husky whisper and he spoke against her lips. "Touching you pleases me. Let me show you."

His lips pressed against hers urgently; his tongue slipped

inside her mouth to plunder the sweet moistness within. She moaned and twisted against him. He finished undressing her, and a tremor shook her body as his hands caressed her from thigh to shoulder, then back again. He tore his lips from hers to let his eyes make the same journey.

"You're so beautiful." His whispers were a warm mist over her skin. "I've got to have you, Jordan. I've got to make you mine."

A fire had been steadily building deep within her, but at his words, she felt it leap and race through her veins until her body seemed consumed by it. He pulled away for a moment to rid himself of his clothes and she reached out frantically to assist him. Moments later he came back to her, and she reveled in the sensation of flesh against flesh, hard against soft, man against woman.

She hugged him to her with a fierce strength she hadn't known she possessed. She wanted to hold him and go on holding him forever. How could she have ever thought this was wrong? If anything in this world was ever right, loving Lance and being loved by Lance was it. She wanted it all . . . and she wanted it now. Arching her body into his, she let her motions convey her yearning, and was rewarded by his answering thrust.

Easing her legs apart, he made a place for himself against the whisper softness of her thighs and, resting on his elbows, settled on top of her. But he hesitated at taking the final step to complete their union.

Cradling her face in his hands, he stilled her movements. "Jordan, it's been a long time since you've made love with a man. I don't want to hurt you. It will be almost like the first time all over again."

She brushed her lips against his mouth and lay back to gaze up into the depths of his dark eyes. "This will be the first time I've made love, Lance. Sex doesn't count. You won't hurt me. I'm just glad my first time's with you."

He moaned as he buried his lips in the curve of her neck,

and she arched beneath him, clutching him to her. He took her then, coming to her slowly, gently, carefully, but completely.

Breath rushed from her body. The feeling was too wonderful to be sustained, too exquisite for mere words. And when he moved against her, slowly at first, but with ever-increasing speed and power, she gloried in the heat and passion that fused their bodies together.

Nothing could be more wonderful than this, she thought, wrapped in his arms, her body joined to his. She could ask nothing more from life than to extend this moment to eternity.

Then even that thought was swept away, and they were trembling together as they climbed the final peak of ecstasy, and the night exploded around them.

11

I don't suppose you'd let me spend the night in your room tonight," Lance said a few hours later.

They were standing in the hallway outside her bedroom, and Jordan glanced around anxiously, fearful that someone would overhear their conversation.

"I don't think that's a good idea," she answered. "It's not that I don't want to be with you, it's just that this is your parents' home, and I'd hate for them to think that we . . . well, you know what I mean."

The Rutledges were home when she and Lance returned from their picnic, and Jordan had felt sixteen and caught in the act when she and Lance had walked in with their hair mussed and their clothes wrinkled to find Dorothy and Matthew seated at the kitchen table drinking coffee. The older couple had graciously turned a blind eye to their son's and guest's appearance, politely inquiring if they'd had a nice evening and offering to share their coffee.

And while Jordan told herself she was thirty years old and above anyone's censure, she still felt uncomfortable.

Lance laughed at her nervousness. "I doubt they'd be shocked, and if they were, they might as well get used to it. I plan to make love to you very often in the future." He leaned forward to lay a soft kiss on her forehead. "But I don't want you to feel uncomfortable. I want our love to be perfect for you in every way."

"Oh, Lance. You make me feel like such an idiot." She closed her eyes and leaned against him. "I wish I could be more clever and sophisticated for you. You deserve someone more experienced, more—"

"I deserve you," he said, and there was a note of finality in his voice. "I don't want anyone but you." He pushed her back so he could look down into her face. "And I haven't wanted anyone but you since that first night I met you."

Standing on tiptoe, she kissed him gently. "I wanted you, too," she admitted. "I was just slower to realize it than you were."

"And now that you have?"

"You're stuck with me." A sudden shyness overcame her. "Tonight was beautiful, Lance. I didn't know . . . I had no idea it could be like that. There really are no words to describe the feeling. . . . Thank you."

"Thank you," he said, his voice husky and unbelievably humble. "You make me grateful I'm a man."

Nothing he might have said at that moment could have pleased her more. She closed her eyes to savor the sweetness of the moment, then hurriedly opened them as she was briefly but thoroughly kissed and pushed toward her bedroom.

"Go to bed, honey, before I forget my good intentions." He brushed another kiss across her lips, then stepped away from her. "And lock your door, Jordan. I'm not good at handling temptation."

She watched him until he disappeared around the corner in the hall before turning into her own room. She brushed her teeth and washed her face with a secret, womanly smile curving her lips. He'd mouthed, I love you, just before stepping out of sight, and she hugged those precious words to her as she went about her nightly routine.

A miracle had happened to her tonight. A wonderful, healing miracle had transformed her from a woman living in a shell to a woman living in love. Lance had given her that love. He'd given her peace and joy and satisfaction that she'd never known existed. And in that giving, he had taken away the fear and pain of another lifetime. She felt joyously reborn.

She pulled her nightgown over her head and leaned forward to stare at herself in the mirror. My God! She even looked different. Her cheeks were flushed, her eyes bright. And that smile—only a woman in love could wear such a smile, she thought happily.

I love you, Lance Rutledge. You've changed my life and I will—

Her cheeks suddenly paled. Lance had given her so much. He'd given her tenderness and gentleness, passion and ecstasy, comfort and honesty. And what had she given him? She hadn't even told him she loved him.

Without giving herself time to think about it, she scooped up her robe and threw it over her nightgown. There were some things that shouldn't be left undone, and this was one of them.

She stepped quietly into the hallway, easing her door closed behind her. She felt like a sneak, but forced herself to go on, praying that everyone else would be in bed. She had no legitimate excuse to be prowling the halls at this time of night. She had her own private bath, and the kitchen was in the opposite direction.

She'd hardly gone ten steps, when a shadow rounded the corner ahead of her. They both stopped, surprised, then ran into each other's arms, holding on as though it had been days instead of minutes since their last meeting.

"What are you doing here?" she whispered when he freed her mouth and she could speak.

"I couldn't stay away. I know I promised, but I couldn't stand it," Lance told her. "What are you doing here?"

"I couldn't stand it, either. I forgot to tell you I love you."

"Oh, God." His eyes briefly closed and he rested his forehead against hers. "I already knew. You would never have made love with me if you didn't, but it's good to hear you say it."

His lips captured hers in a kiss that was almost reverent, and it was several moments before either of them remembered where they were.

It was Lance who recovered first. "We can't stand out here like this. With our luck, someone will come along." He flashed her a wicked grin. "Which will it be, babe? Your place or mine?"

Jordan awoke the next morning to bright sunlight, sore muscles and the best pillow she'd ever slept on . . . if you didn't count the hairs that tickled your nose or the fact that it moved around occasionally, she thought happily.

She snuggled closer to Lance's side, letting her body curve intimately into his, her head on his shoulder, her arm across his chest. She was pleased at how snugly she fit against his body, as though it had been made for her. Then she thought of last night and decided that perhaps it had.

Lance was lying on his back, still asleep, and she took advantage of the opportunity to study him at her leisure. His body was hard, all muscle and bone, and she slowly drew her hand across the flat planes of his chest, delighting in the sensual feel of crisp hair and smooth skin under her palm. The sheet had worked down past his waist, and she could see that the tan she'd admired before did not end in a pale line around his hips. By curling her toes into the sheet and pulling gently, she was able to lower the covering farther, baring more of the bronzed skin for her inspection, and she discovered that the brown went all the way to his toes.

She bent her knee and allowed her leg to slide gently over his. Her skin seemed pale against his, and the slenderness of her limbs compared to the muscular strength of his made her feel fragile and feminine, a feeling intensified by a more intimate part of his anatomy.

It had been a long night. A night of loving and sharing. She sighed and stretched in total contentment. Nothing she'd ever known before could have prepared her for the beauty and the pleasure Lance had brought to her—not only on the physical level but also on another level, a level where hearts and minds, souls and spirits blended in natural harmony and joyous accord.

She was in love—sweet, wonderful, unexpected love. She still couldn't believe it. Other people fell in love; she'd never expected it to happen to her. Her arms ached to tighten around Lance's body and squeeze this beautiful man who had performed a life-giving miracle, but fear of waking him kept her still. For the moment, she was content to lie beside him and enjoy the luxury of being able to observe him, touch him, love him.

She closed her eyes and buried her face deeper in Lance's shoulder. He smelled clean and male, and she smiled at the thought that even his scent could arouse her.

She lifted her head and began nuzzling the tender skin just below Lance's ear. Her fingers trailed lightly down his rib cage and, even in sleep, she felt his quiver of response. Her hand slid lower, over the hard, flat lines of his stomach, down to the smoother skin at the side of his hip, and on to the part of him that proved him undisputably male. Her teeth sank gently into his earlobe as her hand closed around him.

He was instantly awake. As his eyes opened, she leaned over him, pressing her lips against his, tantalizing him with the tip of her tongue and nip of her teeth. His answer was a low groan deep in his throat.

His response pleased her. Under her hand, she could feel his heart pumping wildly as his night-cooled blood began to heat and race. Beneath her lips, his mouth opened convulsively. She took advantage and slipped her tongue inside to tease and tempt and conquer his. He quickly conceded the battle.

Her hands were hungry on his body, and her mouth followed their lead, tormenting him until he cried out for mercy, but she gave none. For him, she was tempest, thunder, lightning and fire, and she gave all she had to give, needing to return the almost intolerable pleasure he'd given her.

But Lance could not remain an inactive recipient. His hands began a magic journey of their own that soon had her throbbing, pulsing. He pulled her mouth back to his impatiently.

He levered his body up as though to roll her under him, but she shifted her weight and, amazed at her own daring, straddled him instead. She grew bolder. Leaning into his chest, she pressed her lips against the warm skin at the base of his throat and was rewarded with his low-pitched murmur. His hands gripped her hips as his own arched beneath her.

"My God, Jordan, I'm dying. Do something. Put me out of my misery."

A thrill of pure pleasure shot through her body at his pleading, and she was amazed at her own power. Never had she experienced such a heady sensation of mastery and control, but at the same instant she realized that her true desire was not to dominate Lance, but to please him and pleasure him.

She slid down his taut, twisting body, and took him inside her with a sigh of sweet triumph. She felt his body tremble beneath hers, then his arms reached up to hold her, secure her, as his hips surged upward in mute appeal. She met his thrust with a rhythm of her own, and soon they were rocketing through space, headed to a world of their own making. They reached it as the first delicious shivers of release washed over their sweat-slickened bodies.

His hand on the nape of her neck pulled her mouth down to his as the first ripples of pleasure pulsed through her body, and he took her shuddering gasps of fulfillment into his mouth as she collapsed against him. She could feel tremors of emotion quake through the body below hers, and she smiled in satisfaction when he whispered her name.

They held on to each other for the long moments it took their breathing to return to normal. And even when her body had calmed, Jordan couldn't find the initiative to move. She was too happy and content to be disturbed and raised her head to look down at Lance, hoping to see that his reaction was the same.

"Good morning," she said, almost shyly. "I'm sorry I woke you."

"Oh, feel free, anytime." His smile flowed over her. "You're better than an alarm clock any day." He kissed her lightly, and an overwhelming surge of love flowed through her veins, so sweet and so strong, that it almost took her breath away. She buried her face in his neck and clung tightly to his shoulders.

Gentle hands held her away so that he could see her face. "Hey, what's this, insatiable woman? Can't leave me alone, can you."

She shook her head and tears shimmered in her eyes. "I've been such a fool, Lance. I've wasted so much time."

"Don't be silly." He tightened his hold. "We've got forever." He rolled over and pinned her beneath him. "Jordan, what's past is past. Our lives start today—together. Nothing else matters, except you and me. Now come on. You're supposed to be happy."

She framed his face between her hands and stared into the somber depths of his dark eyes. "I am happy. I'm ecstatic! Can't you tell?"

"No regrets?"

This she could answer honestly. "No regrets."

"Love me?"

Even more honestly. "I love you, Lance Rutledge."

"Wanna show me?"

Her arms slid around his neck and she pulled his mouth

down to hers. "I'll be happy to give you a demonstration anytime."

"And you'll marry me?"

There was no hesitation. "Is tomorrow soon enough?"

He let out a breath he hadn't realized he was holding. "No, but it will have to do." He gave her a deep kiss before turning serious. "I know we'll have to make adjustments, Jordan, but I'll try to make you happy."

"I'm happy now."

He kissed her again. "Most of my work is in California, but I know you don't want to give up your house in Ruidoso. We'll work something out where we can use both houses. And we can work together sometimes. And when I have to travel, you can come with me. And—"

She laid a finger across his lips. "Lance, I don't care where we live. I don't care what we do, as long as we're together."

"You can bet on that, sweetheart. I'm not ever letting you out of my sight again."

"Promise?"

"Promise."

"And we'll have kids?"

"A whole house full, if that's what you want."

One more question and she'd be satisfied. "Partners?"

"Forever."

His lips sealed the pledge.

For the woman who expects a little more out of love, get Silhouette Special Edition.

Take 4 books free — no strings attached.

If you yearn to experience more passion and pleasure in your romance reading ... to share even the most private moments of romance and sensual love between spirited heroines and their ardent lovers, then Silhouette Special Edition has everything you've been looking for.

Get 6 books each month before they are available anywhere else!

Act now and we'll send you four exciting Silhouette Special Edition romance novels. They're our gift to introduce you to our convenient home subscription service. Every month, we'll send you six new passion-filled Special Edition books. Look them over for 15 days. If you keep them, pay just $11.70 for all six. Or return them at no charge.

We'll mail your books to you *two full months before they are available* anywhere else. Plus, with every shipment, you'll receive the Silhouette Books Newsletter absolutely free. *And with Silhouette Special Edition there are never any shipping or handling charges.*

Mail the coupon today to get your four free books — and more romance than you ever bargained for.

Silhouette Special Edition is a service mark and a registered trademark.

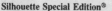

MAIL COUPON TODAY